Give a group of politicians and scientists and some military people too much funding and free rein and they can go crazy or make those they control crazy. The search for the perfect fighting soldier for the nation continues as volunteers are pushed past the standards of normal military basic training. What could be next? When a few soldiers train and go beyond what's normal, they become a threat to everyone — except one woman.

This book is a work of fiction. Names, characters, places, and incidents either are products of the author's imagination or are used fictitiously. Any resemblance to actual events or locales or persons, living or dead, is entirely coincidental.

The Voice In The Darkness
Copyright © 2023 M. Garnet
ISBN: 978-1-4874-3896-8
Cover art by SudaGraphics Inc

Published by eXtasy Books Inc

Look for us online at:
www.eXtasybooks.com

The Voice In The Darkness

By

M. Garnet

Dedication

To all my friends who edit my stories and make sure I get the words and punctuations correct and it makes me a good writer as well as an author. Once again I also had to reach out to some special family members who had the experience to give me some details about the military. I thank you for your help and your service, Ric and Rob.

A special thanks to my IT artist for the great covers she designs for me. SudaGraphics, Inc. Covers do sell books.

PROLOGUE

Sitting among the serious-looking men in the military tent, Sara felt uncomfortable, but not in danger. She understood that they were Army Criminal Investigation Division (CID) personnel and they wanted to question her about an enormous hole in the ground on what had once been a large Army laboratory site.

Sara had overheard the men saying that they wanted some answers before the ATF and the FBI showed up to try to take over what was their job. "After all"—one of the men frowned as he looked out of the large tent they were in—"this is an Army camp and not any of their business."

Fighting a smile, it was as if Sara smelled the testosterone in this area. It wasn't because they were male; it was because they were Army. They were closing ranks. They were not only Army, they were CID. They were like tomcats putting down their scents.

Well, she was here to answer their questions, and that was what she would do, but she would not volunteer information.

One of the older men sat down across from her on the temporary table.

"Okay, Miss Donaldson. I am Captain Sornson. I want to thank you for coming forward. I understand you have a close relationship with Lt. Michelson and must feel relieved to have received a contact from him to find out that he and some of his friends survived what happened up here on the mesa."

Not thinking that his statement required an answer, Sara just nodded.

"Miss Donaldson, do you know what happened up here with this explosion?"

"No, sir. I was down below the mountain and didn't even know that something had happened."

The man looked at some papers and then returned his eyes to her. "We are told the effect of the shake was felt all the way down to highway fifty-one. You didn't feel it?"

"No, sir."

Now the Captain looked around at the other men standing around him. There didn't seem to be any help from them, so he looked back at her.

"Do you or the people of Benson know what was going on up here in the labs?"

"No, sir. There were rumors." The Captain leaned forward, and she thought she'd better add something just to give some feeling that she was cooperating and not keeping secrets, even though she was holding one big confidence.

"Sir, there was always a bunch of guesses. They always seemed silly to me, yet we all worried. There were rumors that they were building weapons or missiles. Some people thought they were making new poisons, and younger people had guessed they were building robots. It was all talk without any tangible proof."

"Sir, some standard black SUVs have just approached the front gate."

"Damn." The Captain started putting the papers away. "Miss Donaldson, I think you need to go back to your friend. We are about to be infested by all kinds of initials. FBI and ATF. Thank you for your help."

Sara nodded and silently thanked him for not asking her about a voice in the darkness. In her silence, her eyes wandered to the mile wide hole that had appeared mysteriously where once had been laboratory buildings. Everything was gone without a trace.

Being escorted back to her *friends* gave her a couple of moments to reflect on how this mess had started out so innocently, with her making a simple move from Florida to Colorado.

Chapter One

When Sara answered the ad for a bookkeeper in a small town outside of Denver, she had visions of working at a ski resort and enjoying the clear air in the slow short summer months. It would be a different life than the one she had in Florida, and she was anxious to start a new career and a different life.

Being computer literate, Sara spent a lot of time researching the Denver area and thought she understood the existence she was moving into—mountains and new views and colder weather.

When her mom died and the bank repo'd the small house, Sara felt she'd needed a change. She had a decent job and could afford to rent or maybe buy a modest condo, but she felt lost and just needed something different. She went through all her mother's papers and found that her mother had spent so much on charities and given all her retirement income away for years.

The bank was right in taking the old small house, as mom hadn't made a payment in months. She hadn't even opened the last few notices from the bank and other companies that demanded payments. Sara did pay off some of the accumulated debt, and that wiped out Sara's small savings.

With nothing left but some old furniture and mom's out-of-date clothes, Sara moved into a month-to-month apartment and nodded her head at all the sympathy from her fellow workers. It was definitely time for a change, a significant difference. She turned to the Internet and looked for out-of-state jobs.

There were legitimate large sites where one could put out a resume or where companies advertised for employees with criteria for certain positions. There she saw a need for a bookkeeper, experience necessary, in Benson, Colorado.

After days of Internet chat, phone calls, and email contacts, Sara had a new job with a thirty day trial that included that she pay her way to the site, but if it didn't work out, she'd be paid for a return trip to Denver and three nights at Ramada.

Fortunately, both Tampa and Denver were big airports, so there were direct flights. Sara knew how to travel. She went with one bag she took on with her and shipped everything else she wanted by FedEx to get there the next day with a hold at the FedEx office in Denver. There would be a small additional charge, but she could either pick it up there later or have it sent on to another address. It was cheaper than the new airlines' baggage charges and better than the possibility of lost luggage.

Having three charge cards with large open balances, she intended to buy clothes that were suitable for the weather in Colorado once she was settled. It was all worked out in her neat rows of thoughts, just as she liked her life, just as she liked numbers.

The new so-called *best American Airport* in Denver started to warn her things were not going smoothly. This enormous development, underwritten by US taxpayer funds, required a lot of walking, with many shops that were either not open or not being used by the travelers.

Compared to the many tourists, visitors, and passengers moving through Tampa, this Denver space seemed lonely and even had echoes. Oh, it was attractive and clean, but still not used to its full purpose. It took as long to walk, ride and walk and retrieve luggage, and walk to get the transports into Denver, as half the airplane ride from Tampa. *Oh, and don't forget the special long ride into Denver since the airport was originally built far away on farmland.*

As was known to happen, traffic, homes, and businesses had grown out towards the airport, but most travelers were heading to the downtown area, like Sara. From there she could get a cheap rental with the GPS that would lead her up to Benson.

It was Tuesday, and all businesses were up and running, so she made a quick call to her new employer to let him know she was coming in. Now her neat plans got worse. Malcom informed her it would take her most of eight hours to reach Benson. He didn't recommend driving in the mountains at night, so he thought she should wait until morning to start.

Parking her rental car at a chain motel, she ate the free breakfast the next morning and even took a muffin in a paper napkin with her. At the desk, as she checked out, she requested two bottles of water and was pleased when they did not add it to her bill. Nice.

The beautiful clean city of Denver was soon behind her as she headed up into the mountains. For the first couple of hours, the road was the standard four-lane highway, but as it began to move around and turn in sharper curves, it became a broad two-lane highway with strange pull-overs every few miles. She needed to do some research on what she was seeing after she got located and brought up her laptop.

Her employer, Malcom Brown, had told her he'd obtained a room for her in the only long-term rental in town. He said there were Bed and Breakfast homes and rooms above the bar, but he didn't recommend it. He assured her Mrs. Rokowski would take good care of her. Evidently, Mrs. Rokowski owned a long-term rental.

Sara had stopped by a local FedEx office before starting up into the mountains and gave the address of the room to forward her packages. Now on the narrow highway with the switch-backs, she wondered how a FedEx truck could make the same trip.

There were a couple of good things about the ride up the mountain. There wasn't much traffic, and the air that came through Sara's open windows was pure. She ate the muffin at noon and hoped to find a gas station. She had plenty of fuel in the small rental, but she also had a lot of fuel in her bladder.

Finally, in one of the wide pull-overs, she went to the other side and stepped over the metal railing to walk into the forest and find a place to do what ancient people had done. At last, she was ready to continue up the mountain.

Even the efficient little car might have a fuel problem, as it took more effort to move upward on the gentle back and forth highway. Sara also found that the road seemed to get narrower. She did notice there were small dirt roads that took off directly up a jutting climb, often with a large mailbox by the paved highway. So these were probably driveways for some homes.

Just about the time when her stomach was groaning and her bladder was objecting to any more water, the highway gradually leveled and widened. There were speed signs and finally a city sign announcing BENSON POPULATION 15,714.

Sara shook her head as she wondered who counted the population. The number looked like it had been erased and changed recently. She approved, as she loved numbers to be accurate. Driving passed the first few buildings, she began to understand this was not a ski resort.

One of the stores was closed, another had an Out Of Business sign on the front door, and across the wide street was a garage with self-serve gas pumps also with the lights turned off. It was only seven in the evening, but the town was shutting down.

She did see a small bank and finally a side street that she had been instructed to take to find the rental home. This small town had normal lights along the sidewalks, although some buildings also had lights on the front. The rental house had several, so it was easy to park in front and take her roll-on up the steps to the quaint wide porch, then open the screen door.

The inner door opened to announce her attendance with a loud tingling overhead bell. Within a short time, an attractive woman only about ten years older than Sara came from the back of the home.

"Hello, I am Rose Rokowski, and you must be my new tenant, Sara Donaldson." The small woman held out a welcoming hand that made Sara feel comfortable after driving up the strange highway and finding the run-down old town.

That handshake was the start of a good friendship, and it took Sara a month to get the small office books into shape. Malcom did have an active business, but most of it was from outside people who had locations in the forests and distant farms. Malcom was the only CPA short of driving down the long road to Denver.

He did a lot of his business on the Internet and was one of those types of people who needed to work without outside disturbances. His small office was made up of a front entry waiting room with a long wide hallway that went back down the center. Off this was an office on each side, one for Malcom and one that was assigned to Sara. The hallway ended in a door that led to a coed bathroom on one side and a utility closet on the other. Finally, the last door at the end of the hallway opened onto a large storage room and the back entry.

This room held cabinets and shelves with the standard office boxes with careful names and dates on the front of each. These were neatly stacked almost to the ceiling, and the cleaning service was expected to dust everything. The sprinkling system was double in this room. The Microsoft spools were stored in a large safe in this storage area, and Malcom was careful to loudly announce that there was never any money in that safe. It was just fireproof for the records.

There was Malcom's elderly Aunt Theresa, who worked at a desk in the reception area, and Sara never could decide what the lady really did on the job besides swap gossip with whoever came in and wait for Malcom. Sara never met with clients.

It was into the third week before she discovered that some of the people talking to Aunt Theresa were just some guys that were retired with nothing to do and stopped in to find out what was going on in town. That was a nice way to say they exchanged gossip.

It was past Tax Date time, so now Malcom was into the reports on people who had filed for a delay. For Sara, this was a learning process, learning the new names and the unique problems for people in the mountains in Colorado. They were very different than the issues of people in flat, damp Florida.

CHAPTER TWO

For the last two days, Malcom had asked Sara to work late to get some reports filed through the Internet on www.Gov.org. It was six-thirty when she walked out the front door, trying to decide what to eat.

"Hey, you are working too hard."

Sara turned with a smile to see Rose leaning against the outside of the window that had Malcom's name and CPA written on it.

Sara turned to the woman. "You know, down in Denver a woman leaning on buildings on dark streets could make some money."

Rose laughed as she straightened up. "How about supper at the bar? They have good hamburgers with their beer."

A fast friendship had grown up between the two ladies. There weren't many single women in the town of Rose's age, and she'd told Sara she'd forgotten how lonely she had been before Sara appeared.

After a couple of hours and a beer and one of the big hamburgers, Sara was soon lying on her back, watching the shadows of the outside tree dance on her walls. She was just about to doze off when she felt a shiver in her body and heard words.

Ouch, Damn. I hate this bunk, it's too short.

Sara jumped upright looking around in the darkness of her room. The voice sounded right next to her. Reaching out a hand, she found the lamp and switched on a light only to find she was alone.

"What the hell is going on? Where are you?"

Oh shit, can you hear me? This is bad.

Sara was almost to the window, thinking someone might be below her room in the yard when she realized the voice was closer. It almost sounded like it was inside her head, and she knew that was impossible.

Nothing more happened as Sara checked the room, even opening the door to look down the quiet hall. She was alone. *Okay.* Bad beer, rich food, and too many long hours with numbers at work led her to begin to hear voices—yep, the high mountain air was getting to her.

Shrugging, she turned off the light and tried to settle down. By morning she had decided it was just a bad dream, and by the end of the week, she had forgotten the whole incident.

It was a Friday, and she was leaving the office at the same time as Malcom's Aunt when four large black SUVs with dark tinted windows went past them at a high speed. Since most of the vehicles in town were older sedans or more often pickup trucks, these vehicles shouted out like trouble.

Aunt Theresa stopped and actually spat in the direction of the dust from the passing high-performance vehicles.

Surprised, Sara laughed. "Theresa, who is that?"

"Government types. Not good." With those few words, the older lady turned and walked away.

Sara just smiled and went across the street as the dust settled. Everyone said that rain was due soon and the dust would disappear along with the warm weather. She made a usual quick stop at the Kwik-Mart for a take-home meal and headed for her apartment that was a room with a bath at the end of the hall. Fortunately for her, Rose had put her on the second floor, as the only tenant on that floor. There were others on the first and third floor, so she had the bath on the second floor all to herself. There was a bath on each level for the renters.

A quick hello to Rose, a hot bath, and a nice salad in her

room meant she was soon ready for bed in her shorts and tee. Rose had told Sara she would want really warm clothes to sleep in once winter set in up here in the mountains. Sara decided she would order some online.

Feeling too tired to even open her computer, she pulled out her pad and brought up a book to read until she fell asleep. She loved the fact that the pad would shut itself off if she didn't turn a page after a set time. She propped it up on the nightstand by her bed and fluffed her pillow. Turning off the light, she settled down and read about three pages before she heard the voice.

Can you hear me like you did the other night?

Sara sat up, but she didn't turn on the light. Okay, she had finally gone over the rim. She heard voices. What would a doctor say about this? What had triggered this—was it the work or the altitude?

I'm sorry. I shouldn't intrude. I'll stop contacting you.

Okay, this is nuts. But Sara did have a heart, even if she was nuts. "Uh, that's okay. You just surprised me. I'm not used to someone who is not here talking to me."

Wait, you are a woman. Fuck, that makes this contact worse.

Now Sara was sitting on the edge of her bed, glad that her door was shut and no one else was on this floor to hear her talk to herself.

"So it's okay to scare a man, but it's wrong to scare a woman. That seems to be a little sexist to me."

This is dangerous. Goodbye

"Wait." Sara wasn't sure who she'd told to wait or even why. She sat still for a moment. "Hello, are you there. It's okay, you can speak to me whenever you want."

There was nothing to hear but the wind outside and the little creaks in the old house. At last, she turned off the book and pad to lie down, certain she wouldn't go to sleep. Of course, when she rolled over, it was morning and her small clock was ringing to wake her.

That day she was a bit distracted at work. Naturally, she didn't make mistakes; she would never allow an error to happen in her numbers. What did happen was she didn't get as much done as usual. No one said anything about her work schedule, so it was only her own demands that were disturbed.

Every night Sara would get ready for bed. Then, lying in the dark, she would call out to the strange voice.

"Hello. It is okay with me for you to talk to me. I will just wait here, and you can contact me."

Nothing happened for too long to count the days or nights. The weather changed fast. The trees turned beautiful colors, but a northern wind with sleet cleaned the limbs almost within days. Fall was not pretty this high up in the mountains. Everyone was changing into bulky clothes, and women no longer wore dresses or skirts.

Sara had her Florida clothes in the bottom two drawers of the big dresser and also into a couple of big plastic containers in the closet. She had picked up her orders from Amazon at the FedEx office. It seemed that FedEx did not deliver up here in this altitude, but their office was within walking distance. They did make arrangements for some locals to bring up their items to the office in town. That was how she'd obtained her original items and now how she began to get some things meant for Colorado weather.

Before it got too cold, Sara made arrangements for the rental company to pick up her car, and as it left, she was sort of stranded. Still, everything she needed was within walking distance in the small run-down town of Benson. They had a taxi service with only one car that the driver, Timmy, often slept in during the daytime on Main Street. Sara supposed for the right price it would be possible to get a ride down to Denver. The taxi's price console had stopped working years ago, as the car had spent a lot of time in the local garage.

She tried to forget the voice in the night and didn't mention it to anyone, even her friend Rose. She began to worry that she had imagined it and was losing her mind after moving away from everything she knew into a strange environment. Perhaps the voice was something she imagined from the love stories she read from the large pad. She changed over to a SciFi story and found an author to follow with ideas far in the future.

Malcom had confirmed that her job was permanent now, perhaps because winter was coming. An opportunity had never arisen to find out what had happened to the last bookkeeper, whose name was in the records that Sara was in charge of, but she did not ask about the man she had replaced.

It was lunchtime at work, and she was passing Theresa's desk on her way out to grab something from across the street. Through the front windows, she saw the mysterious black SUVs go flying by in toward Denver, well over the speed limit.

When she glanced back at Theresa, the old lady was frowning at the vehicles as they drove by.

"Theresa, you know I'm a new-comer. I don't know the history of those black cars. What's the story?"

Theresa huffed. "Bring me back a tuna fish sandwich, and I'll tell you the sad story as we eat."

Hurrying to complete the task, Sara was pleased and surprised. Theresa talked to some old-timers who stopped in to take up space in the chairs in the waiting room. On the other hand, she said little to Sara or any of the younger people on the street, including Rose.

Sitting across from Theresa with her own sandwich and a soda, Sara waited patiently while the older lady spread out a napkin, opened the wrapped sandwich, and brought out a bottle of water.

The lady took a bite and began to talk around her food. "It

was almost ten years ago when some lawyers showed up. Denver folks. They had the names and copies of titles for the land up on the mesa."

She took another bite and a drink of water. "That is a flat area of lots of acreages that was free land for farmers to run cattle. Everyone used it for a long time, even their grandparents, but it turned out that a couple of families actually owned it. So the lawyers made an offer of actual cash, no fuss, just cash, and the people jumped at the cash. Most of the folks up here don't have enough cash to pay for two months food."

It was time to take another bite and a drink of water. This was going to take Theresa a long time to tell, but Sara knew better than to interrupt her. "So within a couple of months, the highway you drove up got repaired. All the holes got repaired, and the passing lanes were added, and the next thing we knew there was all kinds of heavy building equipment coming up the mountain and passing through our town.

"They went up to the mesa and began to clean it up and erect buildings and dig caves for offices back into the cliff — that is, the mountain or back of the mesa. Benson had a hay day. All kinds of rough construction workers were in town needing beer and food.

"Everyone started coming up with ideas to earn money off this new surprise. The bar set up tables on the sidewalk. The stores all sold beer and food late at night. The FedEx was busy, as everyone who lived in Benson ordered items that could be sold to the new workers."

It was time to take another bite and a drink of water. Sara ate and sighed, as she wanted to ask questions. Theresa continued dribbling water. "The workers left with the equipment along with rowdy goodbyes. But before anyone was starting to worry, the next group came, in army trucks and black SUVs.

"The word went out that the mesa was now a unique army

base around a laboratory for unusual research. Okay, everyone smiled, as we all felt the army guys would drink a lot of beer and science geeks would buy a lot of extra clothes for the cold weather."

Now Theresa shook her head as she began to finish her sandwich. She ate without talking and then rolled up the papers and threw them away.

At last Sara had to ask her questions, so she started with what she thought was the obvious one. "What happened?"

"They closed the gates on that big wall they built around the mesa, and no one comes out. There are helicopters that we hear overhead. Now and then we see the black cars whiz past. But no one comes into town.

"We dried up, and one of the better cattle runs was gone."

Finishing her own sandwich, Sara thought about a voice in her head. "So Theresa, what do they do up there?"

"Who knows?" Theresa took a drink. "It could be anything, since there is no way for any of us to see. If one of our rambunctious kids gets too close, the army escorts them off. They could be building missiles, developing new poisons, or making robots. It is all very secret, and Benson is not a part of it. We just got ripped off of some good land."

CHAPTER THREE

For days Sara could not get her conversation with Theresa out of her mind. She talked to Rose about the Army Post, and the story was pretty much the same. Rose was not as bitter, as she hadn't expected anything from life but what it gave her. Rose did tell her the Post had a name on the outside wall. It was called Camp Mesa Training & Medical Center.

Evidently, if you took the newly paved road up to the big wall and metal gates, there was a nice metal sign set into the block wall that proclaimed that name. It didn't really tell the Benson home folks anything. Who was being trained, and what was in the medical section? Still, the helicopters came and went, big ones, even in the bad weather with heavy snow.

Periodically the black SUVs also tore down or up to the mountain, never slowing down and never stopping for a beer or a sandwich. No one ever needed gas from the one station in Benson.

The same story with different frowns was told to Sara from folks in the town. Sam, the kid at the market, Malcom added his short version, but it was all the same. A mysterious military base doing unknown something was on good land outside of town.

It was October, and in this high altitude, it was deep winter. Snow was a permanent feature with piles of older dirty patches being covered by new. Sara was living in her warm lined boots and a puffy vest, even in the office. Everyone seemed to accept this as a normal way to dress. Halloween decorations began to show up here and there, but it was simple. The town was dying.

Sara had found a SciFi author she really liked because he built good characters into his futuristic stories with a touch of love. Yep, people still fell in love thousands of years ahead.

Reaching for a glass of water on the nightstand, Sara realized she was whispering the words as she read them, and it made her mouth dry.

He's going to convince the Commander to send the shuttle out to save her.

Sara set upright in the bed. The only light in the room was from the reading pad. "You're back."

You have such a strong mental source. I am drawn to you reading this book. I should stay away to protect you.

Looking around in the dark room and listening to the quiet house, Sara decided just to whisper, as she didn't want anyone to hear her talking to herself.

"What are you protecting me from?"

Please read some more of the story.

Sara knew a couple of real facts. She was not going crazy, and the voice was inside her head. Okay, she was reading science fiction, and she knew what mental telepathy was supposed to be, but she didn't think it was real. Still, she knew this voice was inside her head, and right now, she felt strong enough to believe she was not making it up, it was real.

Picking up the pad, Sara returned to her story and whispered as she read. Then in the middle, she whispered, "Where are you at?"

I am in the camp. I don't think we should get too close.

Sara waited a moment, not reading, just giving him time to think or whatever it was that he did.

Where are you?

"I am in Benson," Sara whispered.

So a couple of miles apart, that is the farthest that I have reached someone. Especially someone not trained. Goodbye.

"Wait, I have questions." Sara realized she had spoken out

loud. She started whispered again. "Hello. I am here waiting. I, uh, there is a lot we can talk about, but you have to be the one to make contact. I will wait."

Settling down in her bed, she waited. It was her alarm that woke her in the morning, not a voice in her head. The next day was her weekly night of beer and hamburgers with Rose.

"You're pretty quiet tonight. Is Malcom working you too hard?"

Smiling, Sara shook her head. Actually, her mind was not on work or even her friend Rose; it was on going home and getting in bed to wait for a voice in the darkness.

"Sara, wake up." Rose nudged her on the shoulder.

"Sorry, Rose. I haven't been sleeping well lately. Maybe this beer will help me relax. Let's cut this evening short. I promise next week will be better."

The girls finished their food and drinks and bundled up to face the cold winds as they walked home. The sidewalks were salted, and Rose kept her steps clean, but it felt good to reach the warm heat of the inside of the rental home. At least Rose had a good furnace.

Now Sara had double thick long-sleeved PJs and three quilts on her bed. Rose warned everyone that the heat was turned down at night to save on cost and the fuel for the possibility of a long winter.

Once in bed with the lights out and the cool of the house setting in, Sara had the pad with its back-light with her, buried under one of the quilts. She was whispering as she read.

I told you they would save the pilot.

"Hi." Sara didn't want to spook him, so she read another page in whispers. "Uh, I sort of missed you." She felt the covers would also hide her whispers, even though she was alone on the second floor.

They have been trying me out on some new projects. I started a fire.

"Was it an accident? The fire, I mean?"

No. It was the project. I had to start a fire behind a steel wall forty feet away.

"That's ridiculous. Did you have a flamethrower?"

It is one of the tricks I can do with my mind. Now they are trying to find how far away I can be to start a fire.

"Wait, you can start a fire just with your mind, like the same way you can talk to me in my mind?" Sara pulled her feet up and was soon tucked into a fetal position.

I am an experiment.

Sara had to think about that for a moment. There were a thousand questions that could follow that statement.

"Are you real, I mean, are you human?" Sara imagined talking to a robot, thinking of what Theresa had said that they might be doing or making at the Camp.

I am Lieutenant Jeffrey Michelson of the US Army.

"Wow. And you are part of an experiment. I am Sara Donaldson, a bookkeeper in Benson. How did you become an experiment?"

I volunteered. It is something soldiers do, we volunteer.

Chapter Four

Numbers were the way Sara found escape. It was a world that could be controlled. She organized the job of posting Malcom's business accounts into a standard system. This meant that each week she took the checking account book from Aunt Theresa, went online, and looked at the company bank account. From these figures, she spent some time assigning the data into the right accounts. Double entry bookkeeping — yes so simple — Sara loved the control of numbers.

Jeff did not contact her every night, and of course, the contact was always from his end. Over the months of the cold winter, she had tried to reach out to him, and it had never seemed to work. But then without any reason, she would almost fall asleep while reading, and he would be there in her mind.

Sara never mentioned it to anyone, because when she thought about what she would say, it all sounded stupid or even crazy. She had visions of spending hours in a doctor's office telling of missing her father, or worse, being in a hospital.

Doing her research, she found that hospitals for people needing help in delusions were very much like resorts. Insurance took care of most of the cost. Sara had her own insurance, paying from her wages when she worked, and from charge cards when she was in between jobs. At present, two of her three cards were open, with only small balances to keep them active.

No, sitting before a doctor or lying around a resort hospital was not going to be in her future, so she kept her secret about her voice in the night. There was one more threat to Sara. Jeff warned her that the people who ran the projects at the mesa Camp would do anything to keep their experiments secret, including arresting and making people seem to disappear.

For Sara, as she gained a semblance of peace in her numbers, she still looked forward to when a voice in the darkness would talk to her. During the daylight, in the air that was so cold it left frost in her nose, she had to wonder why she would like to hear from Jeff.

There was a need inside of Sara to learn more about the distant man who could reach out and talk to her inside her mind. There was the wonder of how they could meet.

The main streets in Benson had to be plowed every day. Doug Jr. ran the local garage and gas station and was paid by the city to keep the streets free for at least one lane during the long winter days. Anyone else could also hire him to clear out private drives and side roads. Doug Jr. had a later pay system so that during the winter people contracted for his service and in the summer they paid him. Rose had him keep her area clear for her old Jeep and anyone else who drove through.

All the teens made money shoveling the walks and steps, and it was cash on delivery. Rose got hers done early, as she always had hot chocolate and fresh baked cookies when the job was done.

Kids did not go house to house for the trick or treating like they did in the beautiful weather in Florida. The weather at night was brutal. Instead, there was a party at the small church basement. Everyone went, even if they didn't belong to the church.

Bundled up and with a fake fur-lined hood pulled down tight, Sara helped Rose take a load of great baked pumpkin bread and cookies they both had decorated with orange icing. The kids would all have sugar overload in the morning.

Sara learned that most of the kids in the area of Benson were homeschooled, sometimes in small groups. There was some schooling in the church. Older children would often stay with a relation down the mountain for the high schools. They returned for the summer to help with the chores or farming. It was the mountain way of life.

It had been several cold nights with Sara tucked into her thickly covered bed when she felt the touch of Jeff.

You finished the other novel. Did it end well?

"I've missed you. Yes, they found the bad guys, and the lovers got together in the end. They flew off into space to find a new enemy."

There was silence around her as if the heavy snow covered even the old house, and it no longer could groan or creak.

"Jeff, tell me something about you."

What do you wish to know?

Sara thought for a moment. Would he really tell her what she wanted to know, things about the Camp? She decided to play it safe. "Well, how about like, how old are you?"

Oh, so you don't want to have an old man inside your head, do you?

She actually heard him chuckle. "So I am twenty-eight. Don't laugh, how old are you?" She wasn't sure why it was so important, but she felt she wanted to know facts, and she needed to start somewhere.

Okay, I am 32, a career military man. I am a 1st Lieutenant, and yes, I volunteered for this experiment. I wanted to help serve my country to protect people like you.

It was a start. "Thanks." She was used to whispering under the heavy quilts. "I am Sara Donaldson, and I work as a bookkeeper and auditor for Brown's CPA Services right here in Benson."

This was when Sara felt they began to become friends. Jeff was no longer a weird voice in her head, but a real man over in the camp who had the ability to whisper to her in the night.

Now there was a short contact each night. Sara began to feel a difference in him. She thought she could tell when he was tired or had done some things in the experiment that he was unhappy he'd performed.

They were careful to stay away from talking about what he did as an experiment and anything connected with the Camp. He was not about to turn traitor and tell her anything that was considered a secret. He also assured her it was for her safety. He was concerned that he was putting her at risk if anyone found out that they were in contact.

Now Sara had a strong reason for not telling anyone in Benson about her night talks. Her evening out with Rose was not as fun as it had been in the past.

"You always seem to be distracted. If I didn't know all the men in Benson, I would say you had a new guy in your life."

Laughing, Sara looked around the room in the friendly local bar. This was the only place in Benson to get drinks except buying six-packs at the market. There were a lot of married couples and some men in groups. In the winter, a lot of the local men grew beards, and as Sara looked around, most of the beards had grey in them.

The young men of Benson left early for good jobs down in Denver. There was no future up in the mountains. The farmland was poor and not very large. The forests had been logged out, and there were no gold in them thar' hills.

High school, college, and jobs were all down below these rough mountains. Once the youth got a taste of that life, it was hard to convince them to return. Oh, they did visit for the holidays, but that became less and less frequent. The FedEx office handled their gifts more than the sons and daughters returned for visits. There was one narrow truck that made the trip. It often followed the narrow four-wheel vehicle that brought the mail on most weekdays. Sometimes, FedEx used the rental services of a farmer coming up in the deep snows.

Smiling, Sara knew Rose was correct, and there were no boyfriends available for her in Benson. Thinking of her job and the numbers, she probably would have turned around and gone back down the twisting highway if it weren't for the night voice.

Making excuses about the work at Brown's, Sara ate the hamburger, but only drank half of the beer. They walked home together, now seeing the Christmas lights glowing in the air that froze in their breaths.

"I didn't think it would snow when it was so cold." Sara drew her hood fake fur up around her mouth and nose.

Rose gave a harsh laugh. "The mountain catches the clouds, and we still get the moisture, or snow in this case, even though it is so cold."

They hurried, careful of the icy spots on the way, and were grateful as the heat hit them when they entered the house. Rose invited Sara for a hot chocolate, but of course, Sara said no and headed for her room. She wanted a hot bath before Rose shut down the heat.

She and Jeff were reading a book together. It was a SciFi and had Marines fighting far into the future that Jeff liked. It also had a love interest that Sara found interesting for her, so they both looked forward to each new chapter.

They both said goodbye, and he was gone. Sara lay on her back with the quilts pulled up to her chin and thought about Jeff. Their time together was really only about twenty to thirty minutes each night that he slipped into her mind. It was also to be noted that he did not come every night; it was sporadic, two or three nights often separating their talks. He never gave a reason for the times of his visits or the times apart.

Not wanting to question him, knowing it might have to do with the Camp, still, she found she was disappointed on the nights he was not with her. Now Sara had a reason to question her sanity for a different reason. Was she becoming attached to a voice in her head?

No, attached wasn't the word. There had to be some other word for what she felt when the thought of Jeff interfered with her numbers. Nothing had ever stopped her numbers, so what was the word? Affection, warmth, intimacy — how could she have that type of feeling for just a voice? Damn, maybe she was going off the edge, and it had just started with a voice.

The next day at work, she brought her laptop with her and did some searching to study about hearing voices, and that led to sites with just too much information. Scanning a couple of the websites provided her with either technical information that was useless or sites that wanted to sell her sleeping aides, including mattresses or pillows.

She did get a couple of pop-up ads for online talk to *Trained Analysis*. Okay, she could use a charge card and try a conversation or two and see what type of bull they were handing out.

Chapter Five

The online talk was a complete waste of money. First, Sara found out that you were charged by the minute. There were some minutes at the beginning of each session that were wasted, as there were the introductions and the claims that absolved them from laws and possible suits.

Sara was assigned to a charming lady who had a calm voice on the computer call. She explained that voices in the night were often strong dreams. She gave Sara all types of things to do to get a better night's sleep and suggested she needed a six-week session paid for in advance, two hours daily.

Sara only had the two one-hour sessions and made sure the site was blocked from charging any additional costs against her card. There was only one doctor in Benson, and in any other place, he would have been retired. She knew better than to talk to him about a voice speaking to her in her head.

Christmas came and went, with Sara actually getting some cards from old friends in Florida. They were the usual silly ones with Santa in shorts on a beach. She bought a couple of cards in the market and sent them out at New Years with thank you notes inside. With Easter, there was another heavy snowstorm that stopped deliveries and closed the highway for four days.

Some type of large unit with a grinder on the front and a blower came out from the camp only as far as the town. Of course, they did not offer to clear the rest of the way for the people on the mountain.

During this winter in the high altitude, Sara lived two lives.

She devoted herself to the numbers in the day, always doing everything perfectly and getting nothing but praise from Malcom.

At night she read her stories and waited for Jeff to come to her. The nights that he was in her mind meant she was in a different world. They shared their lives and their problems. They laughed at the idiots that were around them and was amazed when they found some special person that did something that surprised them.

More and more, Sara looked forward to the feeling she had when Jeff entered her life. She finally admitted that she had emotions for him that she had never felt for anyone else, especially any man. She was absolutely nuts, falling in love with an imaginary man who invaded her sleep to talk to her in her mind. Impossible.

The next evening that she and Rose were at the bar for hamburgers, she ordered extra beers for both of them. They played a game of thinking of names for each of the men in the bar.

"That one is Abraham," Rose said.

"No. That was too easy. I think he is Cedric."

Again it was Rose's turn. "Okay, how about the gut with the silly mustache? I think his mom called him Finley."

"Oh, that's a good one. Ten points." Sara looked around. "Look at the two brothers at the end of the bar. Crawford and Elias."

They worked through the men and couldn't think of a Z name and just decided they would not start on a couple of women who had to be the wives of the guys they came in with to be out of the cold.

By the time they bundled up and walked home, it was close to midnight, and Sara even accepted Rose's invitation to hot chocolate. The two ladies sat in the cold kitchen being warmed by the cups they sipped, as they giggled over their silly game.

She did not feel Jeff in her mind that night or for the next week, as she spent more evenings with Rose. After the first of the year, it was getting into tax season with a lot of farmers and town folk looking to stay out of trouble, but not having made any money in this impoverished area.

The farmers and the residents of this area had a deep resentment of the US government that didn't have anything to do with the Camp. It seemed to Sara that the Camp just made everything worse in the local peoples' attitudes.

Doing Malcom's company books, she saw that he charged less than any CPA that she knew of from Florida for his services. Still, since he was the only one up the mountain, he made good money, enough to pay her and himself and Aunt Theresa good wages and benefits. He had a captive audience . . . well, clients.

As the workload got more substantial and with the weather not breaking from the snow and cold, Sara took some home on her laptop. Late at night, she was under her quilts with the light of the screen working on her data input, totally immersed in something she could control.

I've missed you.

Damn. Sara closed her computer, and it was dark under the warm quilts. "Hello."

Hello. That is all you have to say?

"I've missed you too."

Where have you been?

"Nowhere. With the weather up on this mountain, there is no place to go."

There was silence in her mind, which was really strange.

"Are you still there, Jeff?"

But you were not in bed reading your stories.

Deciding the truth might be the best way, Sara sighed. "Jeff, I got confused and scared."

Are you frightened of me?

"Well, now that you bring it up, you are pretty fearsome. A guy who can start fires without a match and talk to people in their minds from miles away — that seems a bit hair-raising. I don't even know what you look like. Besides that, you work for some very strange government types. People in town tell me that the guys in black have been known to make some kids just disappear."

The lab techies are okay, but the guys running the show are government types I don't trust. I do have confidence in the army men that are on patrol here. I will protect you, and I have some tricks to put out there to make sure no one messes with you.

Laughing quietly, Sara nodded, even though she knew Jeff couldn't see her movements. "You know there is an old movie called *Firestarter*, don't you?"

I never saw many movies, and in here our TV is restricted. What is it about?

"Wait, I am looking it up on my computer." There was now light under her quilt as she brought up her laptop and through a search got a lot of hits on the movie *Firestarter*.

"Oh, I found a good source on it at Wikipedia. Not only that it is a movie made from a book written by Stephen King, but it is also about a young little girl and her father, who both have unusual talents due to something given to the parents. It is one of King's scary but good character written stories. I can download a copy from Amazon, and we can read it together." Sara went to Amazon.

Does this mean you have gotten over your fright of me, and willing to talk at night now and then?

"Shhh, the book is eight dollars and ninety-nine cents. I have a special free subscription with Amazon Prime, but King's books are never free. Still, it's not that much, and it goes on my account and is downloading right now."

It is getting late. Perhaps we should start it tomorrow.

"I think that's a good idea. I promise to go to bed early." Sara actually felt Jeff chuckle in her head.

CHAPTER SIX

With the thought bugging her, on the third night of reading King's exciting novel, Sara asked her question. "Is the Camp you're in like what the situation the girl and her dad found themselves in at that location?"

No. No beautiful bedrooms and horses in a big barn. We are in a normal Army situation with uncluttered barracks and everything square. The lab areas look like lab areas.

"What about men in black suits? We see black SUVs with all the windows dark so that there is no way to see who is inside. Are those the guys that we should worry about?"

They must be just shuffling in more of the lab geeks. We don't see anyone except uniforms. Some have a lot of medals, but nothing for us to worry about. Of course, it's the Army, so the government pays for everything.

"Jeff, I have to call it a night. Speaking of government, we are in the middle of tax season. Night."

Goodnight, lady.

So it went for the next couple of months that the people in Benson called spring. Malcom filed all that he could and put in the proper delays for the rest. That meant they still had a lot of work.

Looking at the walk to work with sleet in her face, Sara understood that spring meant the snow didn't pile up on everything. There was something called black ice in strange spots on the streets and sidewalks. Even the locals would slip or fall.

Then there was a time when the sun was out all day. After

that, the sun would stay out every so often and become a regular partner to everyone. Sara still dressed up in heavy layers, but the mountain people began to go around in only padded vests. They still had knee-high boots, but she decided they probably wore those all year round.

Easter rolled around, and it was warm enough to open the windows and doors during the day. That was when Sara heard the news of the town's only celebration. Founders Day.

From what she heard from the people gossiping with Aunt Theresa, everyone set up tables out in front on that weekend and sold handmade goods and all the local foods and items that had been canned. Beer, whiskey, and even some moonshine would appear both nights, and lights were strung, along with anything that would hold up attachments.

Malcom told Sara that the business was closed without pay on that Friday, so she would have a long weekend. That was okay with her, as Rose drafted her to help with setting up her front porch for the sales of homemade pies.

First, they lined the whole porch with small strings of white lights. Then Rose had brought out small heaters that would be turned on for late at night.

The whole house smelled glorious. The cook and Rose baked pies for a week in advance, and the refrigerator and freezer were overflowing. The smell waking Sara each morning made her want pie and coffee for breakfast each day. It was a good thing she had to walk a lot to get rid of the calories. The cook grumbled about each piece Sara ate as a sale that was lost. Sara began to leave dollar bills on the table after eating.

The big weekend was coming, and farmers were arriving into town to set up their own tables in front of empty and closed buildings or where others, like Malcom, had made arrangements for clients to use the space.

On the Thursday night before the holiday, Sara was ready

when Jeff came into her head.

Sorry I'm late.

"No problem. Nothing exciting happened. The father is getting suspicious. Besides, I wanted to tell you that tomorrow night and Saturday night I probably won't be reading. There . . ."

I know. The town celebrates.

"Oh. Sorry. I guess I just thought you were cut off and didn't realize what was going on in the outside world."

I know a lot more than you realize. In fact, I have a warning for you.

Now Sara sat up in the dark room. The quilts fell away, still covering her pad with the light hidden. She realized that she could hear the noise in the house. Of course, the cook with some help was still baking pies through the night. Now it was really important that no one heard her talking to herself.

She slid back down under the quilts and pulled a pillow up over her head. Lying on her side and ignoring the pad, she spoke in a whisper to Jeff.

"Okay, tell me about your warning."

As a pretense for the celebration, there are going to be some soldiers on so-called furlough on both Friday night and Saturday night. They are really being sent in as spies. There is something weird going on. Be careful. Stay in crowds. Good night.

With that, Jeff was gone. Sara always knew when he was with her, and when he was gone. Damn, there were so many questions she wanted to ask him about the warning and the soldiers. She pushed the pillow away and sat up again. With all the cooking, the house was warm. Perhaps it was also the warmer days.

Sara wondered how she was going to whisper to Jeff with the windows open in summer. She had to find a better way to talk to him, because she wasn't willing to stop her contact with this strange voice in the dark.

Now that she had convinced herself that she wasn't insane,

she was beginning to think that maybe there was some way to help this unusual man. He hadn't asked for any help, but he did seem sad inside; it came through his mind to hers as a feeling, a feeling that projected sadness. *Strange.*

Chapter Seven

Surprised that the celebration started early, Sara was put to work handing out slices of pie to people who were buying breakfast.

At noon, Rose told her to take a couple of hours off and go for a walk and enjoy the other sales sites set up by locals and farmers. It was like stepping back into history. Everything was homemade or home-cooked and canned. There were marvelous old glass jars with the screw on lids full of peaches and jams of different types.

Going from place to place, Sara realized she would end up buying things before the weekend was over. There were hand-carved statues and lovely jewelry made from polished stones.

At last Sara heard the whispers as the Army jeep pulled up and some men climbed out, smiling and pointing around. Two walked over to a stand and began to pick up items.

Watching the clean-cut looking soldiers, Sara needed to warn the locals. She scanned the street, wanting to find the right person to tell her story and get the right reaction. The local cop was talking to some farmers who had set up a table with fresh butter for sale. He also had deputized a couple of youths, but she didn't know these teens, as they were from outside of town.

At last, her gaze fell on the bright colors of Aunt Theresa, who was helping a group of women who had a table full of knitted scarves, mittens, and socks. Sara smiled. as she could always use a long heavy scarf, so she wandered over with more than one goal.

Sara just chatted about the knitted items as she tried a couple of the scarves, explaining she was looking for a long one. Aunt Theresa and another lady began bringing some out from boxes under the table. The knitted items were really lovely and in beautiful colors. The ladies must have worked all winter on the projects.

Choosing one in red and yellow, Sara was digging out the money when someone mentioned the soldiers.

"Well, it's about time they let the boys come into time and spend money."

Aunt Theresa nodded. "Yep, but it will take a lot more than that small group to pay us for the land and time."

Sara took her scarf in a used plastic bag and added her comment. "Oh, I don't know. The guy at the table down the street said they were here to spy on us."

That brought silence to the ladies and some leaning over to look both ways past all the tables.

Theresa walked around her table. "I better go warn others. You just can't trust the government. Ladies, be careful what you say to those soldiers if they come over here."

Smiling to the ladies and taking her item, Sara walked in the opposite direction from the one Theresa was heading. She stopped three booths down at one that was selling honey. It was a farmer from out in the mountainside.

While she held up a small jar, she looked back down the street at Theresa. She just stood that way for a moment until the farmer, anxious for a sale interrupted her.

"A problem, miss?"

"Oh, I'm sorry. I'll take this jar. I was just watching Aunt Theresa. You know her, right? she runs Malcom Brown's office." Sara didn't look up as she dug out a couple of dollars for her purchase.

"Of course. I get my taxes done by Mr. Brown every year.

Is there a problem with Ms. Theresa?"

"I don't think so." Sara handed over the money and added the honey to her scarf bag. "She is warning everyone about the soldiers being sent here to spy and get information on us."

"Damn." The farmer looked down the street, not at Theresa but at the soldiers. "I thought it was strange that they finally came into town. I need to pass the word."

Satisfied that she had settled what she wanted to accomplish, Sara returned to Rose's porch to help sell pieces or whole pies. Rose had also been wandering through the different booths, and like Sara, came back with a used plastic bag, bulging with her purchases.

Rose kissed Sara on the cheek. "Watch the table for us. I want Gretchen to take a break, and I'll make us a couple of sandwiches for lunch." Gretchen was the cook and not only needed to take a break—Sara felt the woman needed a long nap. She had stayed up all night baking.

Since it was after noon, Sara was busy as a lot of people wanted pies or slices for lunch. Fortunately, one end of the long set of tables had slices or pies already cut to serve. The other held the whole pies, some hot and some cold.

When Rose came back, they still did not find time for another hour to relax and eat their lunch. At last Gretchen brought them out coffee and they ate the sandwiches and finished with slices of berry pie.

"We've got this, Gretchen, go and rest. You've done a good job." They had a few more sales before they saw two of the soldiers working their way down from table to booth to porch.

"Now there's trouble." Rose pointed with the slice of pie on the paper plate she was setting out on the row she had started.

"Oh, you mean the soldiers. Aren't they from the Camp?"

"Yep, but everyone knows they're just here to spy on us

and get whatever information they can out of us. Don't even answer any questions, and make sure you don't tell them your right name." Rose looked around at her neighbors, and a couple nodded solemnly. "Everyone is giving a fake name."

"Is that important? Will they check and find out that something is wrong?"

Rose nodded. "We hope so. We hope that they get the message not to mess with us. Call me Merryweather, and I will call you Summer."

When the soldiers came to buy and eat several slices of pie on the steps of the porch, Merryweather took their money while Summer cut more pieces from the fresh ones from the right side of the table. There was no talking from anyone on the porch except between the two soldiers, who soon moved on to the neighbors.

For Sara, the game seemed silly, but she had taken Jeff's word that the soldiers had come to spy and gain information, and she hoped that the warning to the town did its job.

There would be no talking or whispering tonight or for the next couple of nights, and she missed Jeff already, out here in the sunlight with the rich smell of the fruit pies all around her.

Chapter Eight

The lights were gone, and the booths and banners had disappeared. The one time out of the year that the farmers and people of Benson had a celebration had come and gone, and so had a lot of people. Also, the soldiers had disappeared back up to the mesa and behind the gates and big walls.

Spring was over, although Sara would not have called it spring. It was now summer, and the load of work in the office was light. Sara got off early in the afternoon, but Malcom still paid her and Aunt Theresa for the full forty hour week.

Avoiding her reading and any contact with Jeff was important right now because Sara had no privacy. Her windows were open even at night, and there were no heavy quilts to hide under. She felt the brush of his contact but was afraid to answer.

Then one day, looking around her desk, she noticed an old-fashioned recorder on a shelf at one side of the small room that was her office. She smiled and had an idea. She put the recorder into her large shoulder bag, and on the way home, she stopped at the so-called General Store and bought a cheap off-brand iPod that would play back recordings.

She picked up a salad at the market and hoped that the cook had thawed out a pie for dessert. Talking to Rose in the kitchen as she got her piece of pie, she mentioned her load of things from work.

"Rose, I will be dictating or also reading some items that others have written. It probably won't make sense if you hear me. I will try to talk low or whisper because of the windows being open. If I bother anyone, take a broom handle and bang on your ceiling."

Pulling out the wires of all the connections to the recorder and the ear pods, she shrugged her shoulders.

Her landlord laughed. "Sweetheart, I have some wine before a hot bath, and you could bring in a dance band. I would sleep through anything."

So that night when Sara felt the stir of Jeff, she whispered. "Hello."

Were there problems? I kept trying to contact you, but there was no answer.

Sighing, Sara turned on the recorder to something that Malcom had recorded. With that voice in the room, she whispered. "I have to be careful because it is warm and our windows are open. I don't want people to hear me talking to myself."

So have you found a solution, because I have missed our conversations.

"Yes, I am playing a recorder and pretending I have work to do at night. I think it will cover my whispers or make them seem like I am making notes."

Does that mean you can talk for a long time tonight?

"As long as you want. What shall we talk about?"

What is your favorite dessert?

With a chuckle, Sara whispered over the voice on the recorder. "So it's going to be that way, huh? Okay, I have been eating a lot of pie, but my favorite is Ben and Jerry's Black Cherry ice cream."

Oh, one of those fancy ladies, I see.

"So what is your favorite dessert?"

They talked for hours that night and got to know a lot about each other. There were the schools they'd gone to as kids and the friends that had betrayed them. There was the silly first kiss at eleven or ten, and then that subject got changed quickly.

She talked about the pain of losing her mom, and he spoke of not even remembering his parents. She told him she was five foot nine inches and he told her he was six foot two inches.

Her thought was *wow*, and she was thankful that although he could talk to her in her mind, he couldn't read her thoughts.

Whispering, she stated a fact. "As well as we know each other, if you ran into me on the street you would not know me."

It is strange, but if I came into town with a bunch of the soldiers, you would not know which one was me.

"You would have to whisper it in my mind . . .'hey tall girl, I'm the one on the left'."

And then what would you do?

"I would come over and ask you to join me at the Kwik-Mart for some ice cream." Sara giggled.

At that point, her recorder quit. She looked over at the small clock on her nightstand and realized it was almost one in the morning.

"Jeff, we have talked so long that I am afraid that the others in the house might get suspicious. I think I will call it quits. Good night."

Good night, my ice cream princess.

With those strange words, Jeff was gone, and Sara suddenly had a warm feeling in her stomach. She also had a dreaded thought of how hard it was going to be to wake up on time and go to work tomorrow.

Then she smiled, because there was another night to look forward to and a special voice in the night that had called her a princess.

The alarm jerked her out of a deep sleep the next morning, and she made a big production of letting the wires and recorder show as she grabbed a light breakfast in the kitchen. Rose did not call her rental house a Bed and Breakfast, but breakfast was always available for anyone who walked through the kitchen. Gretchen would even take special orders for her custom made omelets.

It was Friday, so Sara wasn't sure that the pretense of work at home would work. She decided to wait until Jeff contacted her and then she would turn on the recordings. But Jeff didn't talk that night, nor anytime for the next week.

On the night that Rose and Sara went to the bar for their usual hamburgers and beer, Rose waited through the silence of their private table as Sara picked at her fries.

"You have a problem, girl. Want to share? I can keep secrets real good, so go ahead and spill whatever is bothering you."

Looking up with a mangled piece of potato in her fingers, Sara scanned around the busy room, seeing the same people. "Sorry, Rose, I had something on my mind. Nothing important, just something missing."

"Yep, I know what's missing, love. Too bad the only love you are likely to find around here is a couple of 'possums back by our porch." Rose laughed. Then she settled down—probably, Sara thought, because her joke had brought no response.

"You know what we need to do? We need to go down to Denver and do some real shopping and hang out at a real bar with some single men under fifty. We can stay overnight in a nice hotel and get a spa treatment."

Sara gave a small smile. "That sounds like a good idea. I haven't been away from Benson since I took the job with Malcom Brown."

"Great." Rose pulled out her phone and made a note on it. "We can get Timmy in his taxi to take us down, and when we are done, we'll get an Uber back up. Next weekend is all ours to be nothing but girls. Bring your check card for cash for the tips to the guys at the dance bar. Ooh, la la."

Now Rose finally got a genuine smile from Sara, and the

plan was put into place.

Timmy had his taxi out in front of Rose's house early Friday afternoon. The ladies had handbags, and each carried large soft carry-on bags with their overnight items. They intended to purchase new clothes on a shopping spree in Denver. At least that was what Rose promised as she had already set up each day after getting a hotel room, spa times, and locations of local stores and bars

CHAPTER NINE

Two very smiling and very tired ladies exited from the Uber after tipping the lady generously. The Uber driver helped them carry all their packages up to the porch and left her business card.

It was almost midnight as the two giggling women shuttled their treasurers into the house. To say that they were comfortable and relaxed would be announcing that the weekend had been successful.

All the shopping, even for items they didn't need, such as tiny thin panties and matching bras, were something they would remember through all the long winter nights. There were even the dollars in the jock pants of a couple of male dancers. Sara couldn't believe she had gotten into the whole charade.

For a couple of nights, she had been too drunk even to miss his brush into her mind. Now, on this first night back in her room with all her new bags and fresh bought goodies, she was still high from the last drinks and the fun to fall asleep and to not think of her stranger.

But Monday morning brought her a hangover, and even the numbers did not clear her mind from missing Jeff. She shifted on her desk chair and realized she had some attraction to this man whom she had never met, but who she knew so much about. He was a soldier that she desperately wanted to meet face to face.

How strange her life was, that she was up on this mountain and found herself needing to make contact with a person she had never met, yet one whose likes and dislikes she knew more about than even the people she worked with or saw every day.

Another week went by with silent nights, and the summer was wearing away. For Sara, her nerves were wearing away as she stayed awake deep into the night, hoping to feel the brush of Jeff. It didn't come, but she did, using her fingers as she thought of the loss of that night voice. Damn, she had become a pervert.

More important was the possibility that she really was insane. Watching TV and looking at the Internet, there were a great many different types of mental problems, more than one that seemed to involve hearing voices.

Looking for something to get her to sleep at night, she went to the Kwik-Mart and bought an over-the-counter liquid that gave a lot of promises on the box and label. All it did was leave her restless and with a headache the next morning.

On the night that was the usual time to go to the local bar, Sara begged off, claiming an upset stomach, and went up to her room. She pulled out her pad and didn't open any of her books, instead going online to find a new one. She found one called The Girl In The Box.

At first, she thought it might just be about a silly teenage girl not agreeing with her mother, but she soon found a deep, dangerous twist in this story. She read until she fell asleep with the pad on her chest.

The next night, finding that she actually looked forward to reading more of the story, Sara took a sandwich and soft drink home and into her room and opened the pad to keep reading the unusual story. In some ways, some unsettling issues were coming up in the story that reminded Sara of Jeff's predicament.

A good author.

Sara jumped in the bed as she realized Jeff was back in her head and was aware of what she was reading. "You can read my mind?"

Hello. No, you were reading out loud, sometimes reading the same over twice. Are you okay?

Looking around at the open window and with no recorder to play, Sara ducked down under the light cover and pulled the two pillows up to form a buffer. "Where have you been? I have missed you. I thought they must have taken you away. You know, transferred you to some other camp or whatever the Army does when they move people."

There has been an incident.

"Oh, are you okay? What happened?"

Keep reading your book. I find the story something I can lose myself in and forget my problems.

Reading a couple of pages in a whisper, Sara stopped. "What are your problems? Can I help? I was so worried when I didn't hear from you for such a long time. I didn't like the silence."

Sara, I think you should think about getting a job down and away from the mountain.

Shocked, Sara couldn't think for a moment. She got up and went to the door to look around the hallway. It seemed the house was quiet with everyone asleep. She closed the window and turned up the speed on the fan, then got back in bed, leaving her legs out from the covers.

"Jeff, if I move, we might not be able to talk. I would miss you. With the time we have been apart for this last week, or so, I have found it painful to wait to hear your voice. I know this is crazy, but I find I have come to look forward to hearing from you. I don't think I want to move away. Why should I?"

There were six of us in this experiment. One didn't survive the first inoculations. Recently another of us was destroyed in an experiment. Now there are only four of us. We are not truly honest with the administrators. It is almost a feeling of survival for us to keep some of our abilities in the dark. In talking to each other, there have been some so-called evaluations that we have not precisely participated in with our full abilities. We feel there is more going on here than what they are telling us.

"Jeff, I don't understand. Why would this affect me to the point that I should move away?

There was silence, but Sara knew that Jeff was still with her. She had a feeling that he was deciding what he might tell her. He had already told her more about the work done to them in the Camp up in the mesa than he probably should, so now he was rethinking his words.

Sara, if there were an accident or a massive explosion up at the Camp, Benson would be totally destroyed.

"Jeff, what kind of weapon have they made up on that mesa that would be so big that it would knock out the mountain and destroy Benson?"

Again there was that strange silence as if Jeff was thinking. She was just about to ask if he was still there when he said one word.

Me.

CHAPTER TEN

Going to work late was a first for Sara, but Aunt Theresa took one look at Sara's face and stopped her tirade. Sara had not slept after Jeff had told her the entire story. She hadn't slept much for any of the nights after, even when he tried to reach her. She ignored him, trying to understand what the world was made of and what kind of men were in this land.

Later in the day, Theresa brought her in some hot tea and found Sara crying at her desk.

"What has happened? Did you get bad news from Florida?

Sara shook her head and tried to straighten her face. "Sorry, Theresa. It is just bad news about a, uh friend." As she reached for the cup of tea, she was shaking so much she knocked the cup out of Theresa's hands.

"Oh my God, I'm so sorry." Sara was immediately down on her knees with some tissue trying to wipe up the mess.

"Sara, stop. You're mixed up and need some rest. Go home. I'll clear it with my nephew and get the janitor to clean this up. The floor needs a good mopping anyways."

Aunt Theresa practically dragged Sara out with her bag over her shoulder and watched as she walked slowly down the sidewalk.

Sara was past the turnoff to Rose's house without noticing, as she moved as much in her thoughts as on her feet. She was running over what Jeff had told her about the work being done in the Camp.

They were building a new type of weapon. One that could not be detected and could take out a large area or number of people, but that would be easy to disguise.

At first, Jeff and the volunteers thought they were going to be changed to become stronger and have abilities to allow them to be the warriors of the future. Then as they were trained to use the abilities inside them, it became obvious to the few men in the process that there was something inside of them that was almost too strong for control.

With the loss of the second of their troop of six, the four had finally demanded answers and withheld cooperation. At last, a non-military man came in to sit down and have a long talk with them.

Jeff said that the man started out by first saying that he would give them the bad news first. He said he was going to answer all of their questions and tell them the whole story of what had been done to them and why. The bad news was that what was done was finished and could not be changed.

He then told the four men he needed to ask them a serious question that would help explain what was done to them and how they could help the United States of America.

Jeff said the man asked if they could go into a room in New York City and stop an atomic bomb from going off, but it would mean their own life, would they be willing to give their life to save New York? They were told to raise their hands if they would give their life to save those million people.

The four men looked around, and all four hands were up. Jeff said the man nodded. The man said *yes because you are good citizens and good Army. Would you do it to save the people of Denver, raise your hand?* Jeff said, of course, all four hands were up high.

Then the man looked up at the ceiling and asked what about Benson that has only fifteen thousand people? But the four hands were still up. *Yes* said the man, *one for the good of many and that is what you four are, each of you is a single weapon that can get into anyplace a man can walk. Then you can give your life and blow up the area around you and wipe out the enemy. It will* be for more than fifteen thousand people, and it will be to save the people of our country.

Jeff said that the man got up and left the room, and for some reason, he left the door open while they just sat there looking at that open doorway.

Sara was in shock, and Jeff had told her that he and his three friends were also in shock. No one had approached them about being trained as weapons or doing strange things. Instead, Jeff said that they had been told to train their bodies in the normal Army way by using the gym or running laps out in the fields inside the wide privacy fence.

All this time, Sara had sat quietly, not asking any questions. Jeff's story was clear and precise and told everything that anyone would want to know. Except Sara didn't want to know. She didn't want to know that the voice she had become fond of was not a nice soldier she would someday meet. No, he was a bomb that someday was going to blow up and take out a lot of other people with him.

She wondered if he glowed in the dark or if his eyes were red like the paintings of Satan. Maybe she should have asked him, but she didn't want to talk to him about small issues. Not little things when he was likely to go somewhere like Iran and take out a square block of terrorists.

No wonder he suggested she consider looking for a job somewhere else. There were four of those bombs up on the mesa. If one could take out such a large area, could four take out Colorado?

If she thought she was insane when she had first heard a voice talking to her in her head, Sara felt she was now in an insane world. Her own government had taken honest men from their service and distorted them into something terrifying.

What was worse in Sara's thoughts was that the four men could not be saved. They were forever destined to be apart from the human race by the process performed on them. Sara wondered if they could be triggered from an outside source or if it was something that they had to do themselves. Were they forced to commit suicide in order to destroy an enemy? She wasn't sure which would be worse, to be at the hands of some lunatic handler who decided that they were in the right place at the right time, or to have to choose the time themselves.

This had to be worse than the men who were told to push the button on the bombs that were dropped on Japan. Did those men or that man understand that the destruction did more than just end the war? Fortunately, those two bombs were the only ones ever dropped on human beings.

If one of these men were used as a detriment, would it take only one to make sure no more would be needed? On the other hand, who would know about the secret weapon? It was not like the bombs in Japan. It did not go up with a large plume of cloud or leave a radioactive glow on the ground to kill others later.

According to Jeff, it was just the use of Earth itself and all the mighty items within a certain center that could be caused to explode. It would cause human bodies to erupt and with them motors and electrical connections. Both wires and items would expand and fire too much power. The gusts of outgoing blasts would level anything, buildings of glass and steel and bricks that would fly from the center, taking down others as they traveled at great speeds.

When it was over, the center would be bare for several miles around, and then the devastation would show in the edges with no way to explain what had caused the destruction. There would be basements exposed as one moved away from the center, but there were no burn marks or traces of explosives. It was a mystery.

Later, from a distance, maybe some cameras would be able to show people going in and out of the area before the tragedy, but nothing to indicate this total annihilation. Nothing that was large enough to carry a bomb or transport enough explosives to cause this great amount of wreckage.

This was what was shown to Sara in her head by the man Jeff, whom she had never met but had come to love. This was done to innocent soldiers by her government that she loved but didn't understand, even with its need to try to protect its people.

Looking around her to see where she was walking, she realized she had walked out of the town on the north end. It was quiet, as there was no traffic. Here the road was new and clear. This was the part built by the contractors for use by the Camp and would lead directly up to the closed large double gates.

Those heavy walls and that security of double gates that prevented entry into the Camp was where Jeff was retained. That was the area where the lab was and where they made bombs. Even the birds had deserted this area, as the only sounds were the wind rustling the trees.

The current of air was cold coming down from the top of the far off peak. Sara hugged herself and turned back to find Rose's house and maybe some leftovers in the kitchen.

"Well, you're finally eating. Sit down at the table while I bring out some soup. A minute in the microwave and we'll have something good in your stomach." It was Gretchen, pushing Sara down in a chair.

Sara was just too tired, both from lack of sleep and in her mind to resist. She sat and stared at her hands until a cup of hot tea was placed in them. The hot tea with honey in it did begin to wake her up as she watched Gretchen pour some hot soup into a giant cup. She was sure that she couldn't eat, but then there was a smell of rich broth, and she exchanged the cup of tea for the cup of soup and blew on it before sipping on the rim of the soup mug.

"This is good." She mumbled out to Gretchen.

"Damn right. Now just sit there and finish that broth and veggies. Afterward, you can go up and get a long hot shower. I promise you will feel better." Gretchen got busy at the stove and ignored Sara, and that was okay with her.

The soup and tea finished. Sara stood for a long time under the hot water and then went with clean clothes to lie on top of the quilts of her bed.

Chapter Eleven

Sara, do you know what teleportation means?

Sitting upright in her bed in the bright daylight, Sara realized she had fallen asleep after relaxing from the food and shower. Now Jeff was in her head and she couldn't talk to him.

"Wait." She spoke out loud. She looked around and grabbed one pillow, then went over to the small closet and went inside to push hanging clothes aside and pull the door closed. It wasn't entirely dark, as there was a small gap under the bottom edge of the door.

With a sigh and thinking her life just couldn't get any more desperate, she slid down on her ass and pulled her knees up to bundle her head into the pillow.

"What do you want, Jeff?"

I find I want to touch you before I die, and we four have found out that the possibility of teleportation is an actuality.

Sara said goodbye to Timmy, who had taken her down the mountain to a motel on the edge of Denver. There she entered the office and paid for two rooms in the one-story edifice, with the rooms located on the end. Since she gave a nice tip and paid in cash, the kid behind the desk didn't ask any questions.

In fact, he didn't ask for IDs as she signed in with a false name. So Margaret Montgomery had passkeys for the two rooms but went only to the last one with her purse and large bag, both over her shoulder.

Now Sara was assured of privacy, as she had the end room, and the room next to hers would not have anyone in it since she had the room key. That had been a suggestion of Jeff when he explained how they might find a way actually to meet.

This was going to be a one-night stay. Jeff had explained that he could find a way to convince his handlers that he was still in the Camp for one night but would need to appear for the breakfast call.

Uncertain what they were going to do when he had said touch, Sara had brought the beautiful underwear from her shopping trip to Denver with Rose. But she was not going to get undressed until she saw him and they talked.

Sitting on the edge of the bed in a musty smelling motel room, Sara wasn't sure what to expect when Jeff entered the room. There wasn't any glowing ball of light; there were no lightning strikes or even the smell of smoke blowing through the small room.

What did happen was suddenly a tall soldier was standing at the end of the bed. It took Sara's breath away for many reasons. One was that she realized this was happening. She was finally meeting Jeff.

Then some of the truth hit her. She was in a small room with a dangerous person. A shiver ran through her body. She had just about decided to make a run for the door when he spoke.

"I knew you would be beautiful."

Just that voice — the soft inflection and the pace of the words were the same as she'd heard so many times within her head at night. This was Jeff, and there was no way that she was going to leave until they had sat down and talked face to face.

She had to see his eyes, his mouth, his hands, so she stood up and slowly took the few steps to the tall man.

"Jeff, you are a bit more than I imagined." She looked up

at the man in the comfortable loose uniform and smiled.

"You look a little shaky, Sara. Let's sit down and just talk for a while."

"Wait." Sara moved back to the nightstand and reached for a couple of standard carryout cups. "I got us some coffee."

The room was a double, and the space between the two beds was only a couple of feet, but the two strange friends sat facing each other. Both seemed a bit embarrassed, yet words were necessary for this first genuine meeting.

Then things changed. Sara asked him if he wanted something to eat, but he shook his head *no* as he moved over beside her. Even the hard bed sank from his big size as she felt the heat from him.

Thinking to herself, she wasn't a stupid teenager, she had a strong idea of what meeting a man in a motel room would lead to, and she had no reservations. Turning sideways to face him, she looked up into those dark eyes.

He slowly lowered his head, and their lips met. It was gentle, and it was magic. His lips were soft, and his tongue was warm as it touched her lips. He pulled back with a tiny lift to one side of his mouth as if to smile.

She realized this was their first true kiss. Tears filled her throat as desire stirred inside her. This was deeper than lust. Something that tasted too much like fear invaded her.

Staring at him, she noticed that he was looking at her, bold and intense, as if memorizing her core's contours. She felt a heat that had nothing to do with the temperature in the room and everything to do with desire and fantasy.

The next kiss was so different. It held desperation she felt the need to get close and resented the clothes that separated them—Jeff seemed to feel the same. Sara was totally in agreement with where the two of them were going. Jeff began to get rid of his boots, and she was sliding out of her slacks.

Her thoughts were wicked, and she was glad he couldn't

read her mind. *Bring on an old-fashioned dose of sex*. As clothes flew away and she even tossed the light undies across the lamp, he lifted her, and they both stretched out on the bed.

For maybe a half-second she was terrified of his bold possession, but then her next thought was *what the hell* and she smiled with contentment. Strong short fingernails teased away her pubic hair and found willing flesh. His other hand settled over her hipbone and pressed her against the mattress.

Sara felt a passion and a need to pull Jeff closer. His wide shoulders and tanned chest were all-male, and she felt she needed him all the way.

"Please, Jeff. Move closer with your body." It was the most that her upbringing would allow her to say, and she raised her body up against him.

There was a hesitation from him, and she felt like hitting him with something. At last, his voice rasped out as he had his own difficulty holding back. "I didn't bring protection."

Now she pushed her groin against his large protuberance that was dropping against her stomach. "Do it. I'll ... oh shit ... I'll get the morning-after pill. Please, Jeff." She reached a hand down, but he was there first.

There was very little problem working that large member in as nature had given them help, with her body so wet. He moved as she was deep in the bed, and then she saw his beautiful face with the short dark hair framing his forehead that was forming a frown, as she knew she was also frowning.

Neither of them was frowning from pain. It was the contraction of the glory as ecstasy was starting to do that strange miracle that brought feelings to sex for humans.

Sara could say nothing more as she grunted and groaned, a scream raking up her throat before bursting free. An orgasm hit her once and then again as Jeff's muscular body jerked in unison.

For both of them, it was an exhausting experience that left

them lying together in a sweaty hard breathing heap together on the bed. It did go through Sara's mind that it was good that these motels built tough solid beds.

Jeff told her they had only this one night, so they didn't sleep. They had sex again and again, but slower and discovering each other, giving them something to remember. Then there was just lying in each other's arms, and she heard his heart with her head on his chest.

He felt hers with his hand in just the right place. They talked out loud without whispering but in the quiet voices of two lovers. They didn't talk of the future or make plans. They just talked of their old lives and of past friends and small personal problems.

They both understood there was no future for them together. He wanted her to move and get as far away from the mesa as she could, and she did ask him if there was any way he could resign and leave the service.

He rose up and looked at her, playing with her hair with one hand. "The government has too much invested in me. It would be like them throwing away that new battleship they just launched. They will want to get some of their investment back. It will be years before they will consider what to do with us unless we accidentally do something."

Sara sighed, knowing what he meant by *accidentally do something*. She looked at what she decided was a body that would decorate any magazine she had seen when going through the grocery store lanes. He had a face that would impress anyone who wanted to buy whatever he wanted to sell.

Still, it wasn't his body or his looks; it was his voice that she realized she'd fallen in love with, as he slowly talked to her in the night. It was his personality that came out with that voice, his care, and his intelligence. All of that had come through when he talked to her in her mind from so far away.

She had more conversations with this voice in the dark

than she had with any other person in her life. They had shared jokes and things that they found that the both of them didn't like, like road hogs, or umbrellas that were never where you needed them and friends who borrowed money.

Jeff said he just told the friend that he was giving him the money and not to pay it back. He explained that way he would not be disappointed if the friend never returned the money. Sara laughed at that suggestion. They both admitted they had never asked a friend for money.

She told of going without lunches, and he told of walking and hitching rides when he couldn't afford gas. No one else would understand why they would find this so funny, but the two of them did know what it all meant.

This was their own time together and probably their last time to talk together, and they had to make the most of it. There was even an hour when they didn't talk but just held each other. She was getting tired, but she refused to close her eyes. Sara didn't want to lose a moment of this night.

Finally, the clock's red numbers said five, and they knew it was almost sun-up outside. They made slow love one last time and stood together in the shower that was inside the bathtub.

Dripping water due to the small cheap towels, they got dressed keeping one of the beds between them. It was as if they were afraid if they touched, perhaps they would not let go again.

Now he was again a soldier in the recognizable multi-toned uniform that she had seen so many times on the news programs. It seemed to make him look even larger and ominous. Yes, he was a warrior.

"Remember, you must move away from the mesa. Go back to Florida or try California. New Mexico might be a good choice. Anywhere away from here, please."

Nodding, Sara fought to keep the tears from flowing. "I

need to go back up to get a few things and quit my job. I won't stay any longer than necessary. Oh, damn, Jeff. This is the worst thing I have ever lived through. I will miss you so much."

It was a good thing that the bed was between them, because it looked like he wanted to hold her one more time. Then just like the way he had come, he was gone.

It was good that he was gone, because Sara spoke. "I love you."

Sara sat in the room for at least two more hours before she had enough control to call for a ride to take her back up to Benson. It was late in the day when she got out of the van in front of Rose's and went in to see her landlord.

Rose was in the kitchen with Gretchen, and she just went ahead and told the news without many details. There was shock on the face of both of women, who had been cooking.

"What happened?" Rose turned to look closely at Sara.

Sara looked around without any answer. "I need to go back to Florida."

Rose frowned. "Oh, honey, I'm so sorry. I knew you were gone all night, but I didn't realize you were checking things out back where you came from. Damn, poor Malcom will have to start training someone all over again. Have you told Aunt Theresa?"

Shaking her head, Sara looked around. "No, I guess I should go down there before they leave. I'll be right back."

Gretchen stepped over. "Hon, its late. They probably left already. I think you need a good meal and some sleep. Go see them first thing tomorrow."

It was easier to allow someone else to make decisions. Sara just collapsed in a kitchen chair and let Rose and Gretchen fix her something to eat.

When Rose helped her up to her room, she just lay across her bed and closed her eyes without removing her clothes.

Rose pulled off Sara's boots and covered her up with a quilt. Sara barely caught the smile on her face before she fell asleep.

Sara woke up to find the room dark and her glowing clock with two fifteen lit in red. She realized she still had on her clothes. Deciding she was awake and uncomfortable, she got up and went down the hall for a quick shower and put on the PJs she had taken with her.

Back in her room, she slipped into bed but didn't sleep as she stared at the ceiling until the sun brightened her room. Getting up, Sara looked around to decide what she was going to take with her and what she would ship. That added another question. Where would she ship anything? She had no idea of where she was going. She would have to find a way to store some things here in Benson.

Finally getting up and finding clothes, she knew she had to face Malcom Brown. It was something she was not looking forward to, but she owed him a face-to-face explanation. Except she didn't know how she could explain anything or what she could say to Malcom since she couldn't talk about Jeff.

On the walk to the office, she decided just to tell everyone it was a personal problem she had to take care of and that it couldn't be put off, as it was serious and dangerous. That was close enough to the truth that Sara felt that she could tell it with all her emotions.

It all seemed simple until Malcom asked for a favor.

"I understand your problem and won't ask any questions. I just need to beg you to stay for two weeks while I get a replacement. We will be going into tax time next year, and I need to have someone who is used to all our strange farmers by that time. Okay?"

It seemed so reasonable that there was no way that Sara felt she could refuse. Besides, it would give her some time to decide what to do with the items she needed to store until she could ship them. She went ahead and sat down at her desk, and it didn't take long for Aunt Theresa to stick her head in the door.

"So, tell me what the problem is that makes you leave us?" Of course, nosey Theresa would think she needed all the information.

"Sorry, Theresa, I can't share it, but I will be okay." Sara just ignored the woman, who was standing in the doorway. Sara clicked away on the computer and then reached over and turned another page over. At last Theresa got the message and, with a huff, left the room. Sara knew the woman would try again later.

That evening, eating a salad she'd bought at the mart, she talked to Rose about where to store the items she would need to ship later.

"I don't see any problem. You can't have that much, as you didn't bring much with you." Rose waved a hand as she talked, eating her own supper. "Go and buy some boxes at the FedEx store and seal them up good. We'll put them up over the car loft and when you get your problem solved, send me a note. I'll take them to FedEx and send them off to you."

Sara waited until Friday and then left work early to stop and pick up some folded boxes to hold the items she would have stored. She told Malcom she could only work until the end of the next week. She decided to travel light and to go somewhere she had never been and no one would know her.

As she thought about all of this, she knew she wasn't the criminal type and had no way of changing her name or history. She would just live her life and move onward and hope for the best. She dug out her computer and did some Google hunting for small towns in the southwest.

Deciding that another location on the edge of a large city just like Benson would be great and probably would have CPA offices, she found a few small southwest towns, then looked up the CPA listings. Next, she updated her resume and sent it out to all of the offices and waited for replies.

So the weekend passed and then she went to work, packed away items, and donated some to the small church. At last, she had the final *girls' night out* with Rose, and they drank too much and shed a few tears and needed help to get back to the house. Timmy took them in his old taxi and didn't charge for the short ride.

It was Thursday, the second to the last day of work for Sara when she heard the rumble of heavy vehicles, even back in her office. Of course, such a racket would draw her and Malcom out to the front windows to watch the parade going down the main street.

Military vehicles of the modified Humvees, most full of soldiers, could be seen moving slowly into the town from the mountain, each bumper to bumper. Every so often army-uniformed men holding weapons would jump off the slow-moving parade to take up positions on the edge of the sidewalks near the street, facing the building and people who were out staring at the Army movements.

"What the hell, is this an invasion?" Aunt Theresa was standing near the door with her hands on her hips, glaring out at the sight.

"Don't be silly, Theresa. This is America, and those are American soldiers. They are here to protect us." Malcom spoke as he moved beside his Aunt.

"Bullshit." It was a growl from Theresa. "Who is going to protect us from them?" Now she had the door partly open and was pointing at the trucks.

Looking at the soldiers and the vehicles, Sara thought about the warning she had gotten from Jeff to get as far away from Benson as possible. She had been afraid of a devastating explosion, but she had not thought of arrest or being held. Could she still leave?

Chapter Twelve

Suddenly things did not look good out on the street. Malcom pulled Theresa back into the office just as a couple had walked up to the soldiers next to the office and were arguing with them.

Evidently, the man and woman just wanted to cross the street, but the soldiers were now asking for IDs and pushing the man back with a weapon. It was not pointed at the man, but it was used as a bar against his chest.

"You two need to get out of here." Malcom turned and motioned for them to follow him. Theresa grabbed her purse from her desk and without asking, Sara ducked in and grabbed hers from behind her desk.

Malcom was already in the storage closet and pulling down one of the standard ceiling ladders. It unfolded from the flat door into two sections that were very solid when it met the floor. The area above was dark.

"Where are we going? We can't just hide. Those guys aren't that stupid." Sara looked around as Theresa started up the ladder.

Malcom smiled and pointed up. "You're going home. It is a shorter walk over the roofs."

Nodding but still looking unsure, Sara followed the older woman. The attic got darker as Malcom pulled the ladder back up into place, but Theresa was already opening something further above and then there was light enough for Sara could see to move around. Surprisingly, the attic had a floor and stored a lot of old client boxes.

"Hurry up, Sara. We need to get out of here and close this uptight." Theresa was pulling herself up and out of the square hole she had opened.

Sara looked up at what was an air vent masquerading as an outlet to the roof. Did all of these locals have some strange way to get out of their buildings for nefarious reasons? The opening was on an angle of the roof, and there was nothing to step on, but Sara figured if Theresa could pull herself up, then Sara would manage.

After struggling, both women were up on the roof, and the air was a little colder up this high. Theresa closed the tilted upturned air vent, trying to be quiet. There was a solid snap as the vent went into place.

Theresa nodded and began walking on the slope of the roof, heading for a section that turned into a flat portion. Sara followed, throwing out one arm to balance herself. She realized it was necessary not to make any noise and not to fall. This was crazy.

They made their way onto the next building, which was taller by only a couple of feet, but it was flat, and now both of them could walk a little faster. There seemed to be some type of markings that Theresa was following. Sara decided it would be smart to walk in the same area that Theresa was, since it looked like Theresa had done this before.

They went up and down several roofs, even finding a metal ladder in place to climb up and over a taller building. On that roof, they found two more people moving back the way they had come from, and there was no speaking, just a nod.

Even up this high and with the cool wind, Sara felt she could smell fear on the people who crept past her as she followed Theresa. What the hell were those soldiers doing in their town? One of the things that worried her was that she had not heard from Jeff.

Sara was also worried about what was going to happen

when they came to an alley or she had to get across a street to go back to Rose's house.

The alley was a surprise. Well, Sara had to say all of this was a surprise. They walked along the end building until they came to what was a bridge. Well, it really wasn't a bridge; it was a metal awning, stretching across the alley between the two buildings. They had to drop down to the awning and then scoot back up to the other building. That was one problem out of the way.

As for dropping onto the back street, Theresa led her down into one of the closed buildings at the end of their route. The building had a vent in the roof and a ladder inside to get down into a dim closed closet. This building had been a furniture store long ago and had gone out of business. They made their way through the dusty rooms, protected from anyone or the soldiers seeing them by the tinted dirty windows.

The back door opened out into a covered area that stored Timmy's taxi. Theresa looked around and then spoke softly to Sara.

"I'm going to tell Timmy that you need to get across the street. He will pull out, and you must stay low on the other side of his car. When he gets close to the bushes on the other side, just move over out of sight and go into the first house. It belongs to the Flints. They will get you over to Rose's. Don't be surprised if someone is coming from the other direction. Everyone is trying to get away from the Army."

Sara nodded. Without falling down or losing her breath, she pulled off the entire trick without a hitch. In the bushes, she heard the soldiers yelling at Timmy. Without looking, the man who used the distraction went back toward Theresa, who was not coming with Sara.

Looking at the old house, she saw a man beside it on a small sidewalk that opened into a side door. He was waving at her, so she stayed crouched over and moved as fast as possible to meet Mr. Flint. This was a gentleman she had never been introduced to before, and all he did was take her through his house and out a back door that faced the back-yard of Rose's larger home.

Leaning against the kitchen door, Sara stood still and wondered what she was supposed to do next. She was still trapped in Benson at Rose's house by a large group of armed soldiers.

Rose came into the kitchen, gathering some items into a tote bag. "Oh good, they got you here."

"Yep, but now what happens?" Sara wasn't that tired, but she was confused.

"You need to go pack a light bag for clothes as if you are going out on a camping trip and dress in solid jeans and boots. We're going out to some farms."

"Who or where . . . I don't understand."

Rose was shoving some big kitchen knives into her tote. "I'll explain as we move. Go get ready."

The sight of the knives shook Sara, and she hurried past Rose to go up the stairs. In her room, she took a moment to get her mind working. She decided she wanted to do this right. She didn't have a big tote, but she did have a backpack and a large cloth bag with a zipper and strong handles.

Her room was crowded with full and partially packed boxes as she had started getting things ready for storage. Actually, she was almost done with that portion of her choices.

She took Rose's advice and looked for items to wear first. Boots, heavy socks, jeans with a solid shirt and a good jacket that was waterproof. What she packed was cold weather underwear and clothes to match what she was wearing.

She went down to the bathroom dand put in only the essentials, deciding one might need sunscreen on a camping trip, but not a lot of make-up. She did grab a small first aid kit that was still full and added this to the cloth bag.

Taking the time to braid her long hair, she grabbed a cloth hat even though her jacket had a pull-up hood. She found a pair of leather gloves. Then, sitting on the bed for a moment, she decided to stop. She knew she would panic and overpack if she didn't just stop and go down to join Rose and find out what she should do next.

Rose was leaning against a cabinet talking to Gretchen. "Oh, here is Sara. Ok, the last tenant is out, so you have a clean slate when asked." Rose looked over at Sara. "Gretchen is staying, but we need to get out before the soldiers find out what is happening to all the residents of Benson."

Rose hooked her big bag over her shoulders, and like Sara, picked up a smaller one as they headed for the back door. If Sara thought the walk over the roofs was an adventure, following Rose was a whole new world for a Florida girl. One didn't go into the swamps or woods in Florida because of the danger. It was not only because of snakes and 'gators. There were all kinds of bushes that could tear your clothes and roots that would turn your ankle. More than that, one step landed you on nice dry land, and the next you were up in water to your knees. There were also bugs the size of birds and birds the size of animals.

Normally if you wanted to take a walk, you went to state parks and walked on wooden paths that were above all the danger. Now Rose just went out to the backyard, and instead of walking into the neighbors that Sara was familiar with, she turned left and headed for some tall trees.

At first, it looked pleasant with tall trees and low bushes to walk around. But within a half-hour, they were deep into the mountainous forest with trees so thick that there was hardly any sun breaking through. What the hell path was Rose following?

When Sara was just about to catch up with her friend to grab her and ask some questions, Rose stopped as a young boy stepped out of the dim shadows of the forest.

"Gramps says we need to get you out of the forest before dark."

Rose nodded and started after the boy. Sara actually had to hurry to keep up with the two. After walking fast and getting hit by shrubs and swinging low limbs, Sara thought that she had to take a break. Just as she was about to say something, the two stopped when they came to a wooden fence.

The kid bent and crawled through, but Rose leaned on the top to boost herself over. Sara shrugged and did the same motions as Rose, and they were in a small pasture. They moved across it but were slowed down as the boy started herding some sheep.

What happened next left Sara with an open mouth as she looked around. They were led into a low barn after the sheep. There were a couple of old stalls, and one of them was set up for a farm office. Before there was any time to examine anything, a man came in and walked over.

"Rose, you're the first that got out. Who is this? She is not a resident."

Rose waved at Sara. "This is Sara Donaldson. She works for Malcom and rents at my house. I don't know why, but I think the Army has an interest in her."

"Well, no problem. You guys can stay here tonight, and we will pass you on down the mountain to the next farm tomorrow." The man turned and gave the boy orders to fence in the sheep. "I'll see that some food is brought out in a while. The rule is after dark stay low or walk on hands and knees."

The man motioned for them to follow him into the office and went to the back wall that held hooks full of ropes, tools, and some things Sara couldn't name. He pulled out what looked like the bottom drawers. They turned into shelves for sleeping.

There was a standard spigot with a bucket under it for

supplying the sheep. It would also give the women a place to clean up. As for the bathroom, there were bushes outside. Sara understood this was a temporary stop. She did have to wonder how long it would take to get down the mountain and into an area where there were police and no Army.

After they settled down inside the barn, looking out through the open door, Sara could — at last — ask some questions.

"Rose, what is this all about? Everyone seems to have expected problems with the Army from the Camp."

Rose smiled as she held a lamb. Sara was getting used to the oily smell of the sheep. "Up here means that everyone is family. They have always stuck together and helped each other even if they don't know what they are fighting. No one knows what they are doing up on the mesa, but the Army is not family and made a mistake when they came into town with weapons. Our people drew together and reacted."

Sara didn't fully understand but was glad to be away from Benson. "Why were the silly instructions about crawling around at night?"

"The Army has night vision and heat registering detectors in their helicopters. They will use them at night to see who is escaping in the dark and have a better chance of catching people. They will soon figure out that about two-thirds of the residents of Benson are gone."

Nodding, Sara understood. Tonight, if she moved, she needed to look like one of the sheep, so low and on all fours. Okay. She planned the rest of what was left of the day out, taking care of her bodily needs before night took over. She was not going to crawl over and use a bucket.

At dusk, after the last good farm meal, the barn doors were shut, and all the doors inside were open. That allowed the sheep to wander around and, for a reason no one could explain to Sara, the sheep wanted to be close to the women, who were tucked into beds that had a final blanket of tinfoil. Really, tinfoil? Where were the aliens? Sara had to snicker, but the noise brought a wet sheep's nose into her face to investigate.

With the inside of the barn warming up, the odor of the sheep was beginning to smell just animal and not pleasant. On the other hand, being captured by the Army from the mesa would not be pleasant either.

Sara wasn't surprised at how fast they fell asleep after the walk through the forest. Trauma had also added to the body being tired, and Sara was shocked when she needed to be shaken by the farm boy to wake up at dawn.

"Miss, we have breakfast ready. After that, it will be time for you guys to move on to the next farm down the mountain."

Sara washed her face and put on fresh underwear before eating. They accepted water bottles and sandwiches along with apples before the boy led them away from the sheep. They were on the trail for about two hours and deep into the dark woods when the boy had them stop.

The two women thought it was to take a break, but in only a couple of minutes, there was some noise. Sara was frightened, wondering if the soldiers had found them. Her mild panic was not warranted as another youth showed up with three people — two women, and a man.

Rose got up and immediately went over to hug the three walkers. She turned and introduced the people to Sara.

"This is Mike and Angela Waterson. Their family owned the property that the church sits on, and they have two other houses in town. This young lady is Gloria Valnet. She is like you, an accountant, and takes care of their business."

Finishing up, Rose introduced Sara to the three newcomers. The decision was that only the new lad would continue taking the five down to the next farm. The other boy was going to return to take care of the sheep and watch for anyone else that came out of Benson.

As they moved quietly through the heavy forest, this escape was not a time for talking or learning about your fellow tourists. After all, they were all in the same boat, getting away from the soldiers. Sara thought that none of them knew the real dangers up in the Camp.

They all stopped around noon, and Sara brought out her cell to check for messages.

"Don't send out any messages or calls. If the Army should be checking, they will find you." Mike nodded and frowned.

Understanding his point, Sara turned off her phone and put it away.

Chapter Thirteen

It took them a week to get down to the Interstate Highway. At this point, they were a total of twelve people with two youngsters. Their guide was a young man who informed them that they could go east to the airport or west into Denver.

Across the highway were several buildings that included a gas station and a restaurant. Both were of the chain variety with cars parked by each, as traffic moved past on the busy main freeway.

"You folks can use your phones now, or there are pay phones at both the station and the café. You can hitch a ride; call Uber or some friends to come to pick you up. The general feeling is that you are out of the long reach of the Camp's pull down here. Good luck."

With that, he looked both ways and jogged across the tarmac. Rose looked over at Sara and asked a question. "What are you going to do? You can come with me, as I have plenty of friends in Denver."

Shaking her head, Sara hefted up her backpack and tote. "No, I think I will hitch a ride out to the airport."

"Want to call Uber? They will get out of here pretty fast."

"No, I don't think so. I don't want to leave any trace, even down here below the mountain. I'm sure I can get a ride, I'll try one of the truckers over at the gas station." Nodding her head, Sara looked at the two sections of the station. One was set up for the fast serve-yourself for the cars and vans to pull in and get gas and run inside for soda or beer. The other side was set up for the big rigs, so that was where she would head, hoping for a lift out east.

Her thoughts were that an eighteen-wheeler who was just going through would not even have questions by the Army about a woman going to the airport. She went first into the station and bought sandwiches, juice, and water along with some apples, all things easy to eat while someone was driving.

Going back out, she took what now were three plastic bags plus her bigger totes and went around to the truckers' side. She didn't know a lot about these rigs or the people that drove them except what she had read in books, so she had to play it by her guts and with her standard smile.

At first, there were a couple of whistles that she ignored as she walked along looking at the front of each of these heavy users of the road. A woman dressed like all the men stepped out from between the shadow of two parked tractors checking out her load.

"Sweetheart, the ho's don't come out until after supper."

Looking at her right in the eye, Sara smiled and didn't react to the insult. "I'm not looking to make money. In fact, I have a small amount." Sara pulled out a fifty and wrapped it in the hand, holding the plastic bag of food and drinks. "I need a ride to the airport without questions."

"Runnin' away?" The female trucker pulled a rag and began wiping her hands.

Sara shook her head. "Running from . . ." She left the sentence unfinished.

The woman straightened up and nodded. "Just a minute." She looked around and then called out. "Hey Big Dog, you're goin' east long, right?"

A big man with a bit of a belly moved away from a group and walked over to the two of them. "What's up, Donald?"

Sara kept her face straight at the names of these two

truckers. So the older guy was Big Dog, and the lady was Donald? She didn't care, as long as she got a safe ride near the airport.

The woman looked at Sara. "Big Dog is an independent, so he's able to take on a ride if he feels like it. This lady needs to get to the airport without questions." With that short statement, Donald nodded and just ducked back down by her truck to bend over and check something out. Evidently, she was through talking.

Holding out the bag of food with the fifty tucked around the handle, Sara looked at the man. "I can contribute some. I just need to get to the airport, and then I'll be able to get a seat on the first flight."

The man made up his mind quickly and took her to a fancy looking truck, where he opened the door and helped her up. Inside she was surprised how nice and clean it was. with comfortable seats and more room than she expected.

The trucker took another fifteen minutes to get the rig ready, and then they were out on the highway. He told her his name was actually Brice Dee and that he had a wife and four children, two in college. He explained he lived in Kentucky and was heading home with a full load that would give him a decent paycheck.

Brice refused the fifty but accepted the food, and it took them four hours to get out to the airport. She expected him to drop her off at the highway as they passed near, but Brice insisted it was nothing to take her into the closer sections at the airport.

It seemed there was a special turn and road for the deliveries, so Brice just followed some box trucks and moved his long unit skillfully around to the area for unloading and told her this was where he would drop her off.

"It is safe here, so all you have to do is go in that well-lit door and tell the guy you are with the truckers and need a quick ride home."

Kissing Brice on the cheek, she tucked the fifty into the unused ashtray and waved goodbye. He would find the money later when he cleaned his truck, being a fuss-budget. She smiled as she entered the double door to find a busy room. It consisted of a casual sitting area, several food and drink dispensers, and a lot of truckers and others who just seemed friendly.

The back wall was the usual counter for handling the customers for flight purchases. The difference from going into a front door of an airport was that this was not broken up into several different sales divisions for the many airlines. It was one woman behind the usual equipment, and behind her was an unusually large electronic board that listed all flights.

Needing to take a moment and get a feel for the whole arrangement, Sara went to a vending machine and purchased bottled water. Shifting her bags to an empty chair, she opened the bottle and looked up at the board. There it was, five down. *Albuquerque New Mexico, Leaving at 7PM, On Time.*

There would be a few hours to hang around, but she felt she was far enough away from the mesa to be safe. She would have to use a credit card, and that would leave a trail, but she had a card that was relatively new and that she had not used yet. It had just been tucked away for emergencies, and that seemed to meet the description of the present circumstances.

The woman behind the counter was efficient and didn't ask many questions. She did explain where Sara needed to go through the back of the connection to the main large echoing airport. There she could take her carry-on totes through to the trams to go out to the sector for her flight and wait in comfort.

A half-hour later she was through the checkpoints and rode the tram to go past the half-closed shops to reach her holding area and wait for her plane. The modern airport paid for by the taxes of the people of America was beautiful, but after all these years still did not have the traffic that it was built to handle. It did set an example for future airports. Hoping she never would see this airport again, she bought a hot sandwich to go with her water and a couple of magazines and a Denver newspaper.

Soon the area around the boarding section was filling up. Since this was Southwest, it was first come first seat and no cost for checking baggage. It made boarding go pretty fast, and she respected this airline.

With a lot of smiles, the airline's staff got everyone on board quickly, and Sara had her large tote overhead and her big bag that she called her purse was stuffed under the seat by her feet. She'd found a seat near the front by the window and settled down to catch a nap. It would be a long flight.

After take-off and settling into the high smooth flight, she was close to sleep with her eyes closed and a silent couple in the seats beside her.

Where are you?

"Jesus," Sara spoke out loud and looked around. The woman next to her glanced over.

"Sorry, I ate something wrong." Sara apologized to the woman and hoped that Jeff would understand. "I'm not used to flying, so I guess I fell asleep, and opening my eyes to find myself on an airplane at this high above the earth kind of upset me."

The woman smiled. "That's okay, honey. You know what they say. Flying is safer than driving on the road."

Good, you got away. Can you tell me where you are going?

Sara nodded. "Yes, flying to New Mexico is faster than driving there. I am sure I will be fine."

I will stop now and see if I can talk to you after you land.

The woman was saying something Sara didn't catch, so she just nodded. "I think I will try to go back to sleep. Thanks."

With her eyes closed, she thought about the fact that Jeff could make contact with her while she was in an airplane above the clouds. This guy could be really scary, except she knew she loved him. There was also the fact that she probably would never see him again.

Part way into the flight, a simple box lunch was passed out, and Sara sat up to accept the offering from the smiling man in the uniform. This led to small talk from the couple.

Finding that she had to tell them something, she pulled up the story that she had told Brice the trucker. She kept it short and without many details. It was just that she was running away from an abusive boyfriend who was also her boss.

Now she was going somewhere she had never been and needed to find a job, preferably in a CPA's office. She also needed to rent a car.

"Oh, honey. Don't rent one from those expensive big companies at the airport." The woman looked at her husband, and he agreed.

"We live in a little suburb just a couple of miles out of town. There is a great little rental place there, and the cars are older, but they are all four-wheelers, which is what you need in New Mexico."

Her husband nodded. "Sure, and there are great small places to rent by the week out there. You can ride with us, and we can introduce you to Merrill. He is fair and rents almost any kind of vehicle."

They talked for a while, and Sara decided the worst that could happen was that these two were just nice people or backyard murderers. She had to take a chance, as this would be her new life, off the grid.

Chapter Fourteen

Her new friends were good for their words, and without meaning to, they helped her hide her trail. There was no card to show a car rental at the airport. What Sara did do was buy a ticket for a one-way trip to Mexico. She smiled to think of one seat on that plane that was going to be empty. It was a waste of funds that she felt might pay off, running away. She showed her passport and listened patiently while the woman at the counter told her to be early so that she could go through the extra procedures that were needed for leaving the country and going into another.

There was a moment when she wondered if she could find a drug addict on the street and for a hundred dollars convince her to take Sara's passport and get out of the country to buy one more fix. She passed on that quickly and rode with her new friends out of town and into the desert country.

Looking out of the rear seat windows, she did not need anyone to tell her she was not in Florida or Colorado. The windows were open, and the dry, warm air took away any moisture that might have formed on her forehead.

They drove through a small town that just popped up out of nowhere in the sandy country along one of the highways. She almost missed the dusty sign with the dints from gunshots and other items hitting it over the years.

The sign read Ojo Caliente, and the small town was as dusty as the road and its sign. Still, as her friends pointed out, only a couple hours from the airport and was on the edge of the Carson National Forest. Of course, a forest in New Mexico was not quite like a forest in Colorado or Florida.

One thing that Sara soon noticed was that Ojo Caliente was large enough to have a bank and several businesses that would draw in the farmers and herders. Maybe there was a CPA's office. Her friends took her behind the line of buildings to what turned out to be a local garage and gas station.

Stopping in front beside the filling tanks, everyone got out so the man could fill up his car and the woman could take Sara in and introduce her to the owner. The woman hugged a big overweight man and then introduced them, explaining that Sara needed a car, a room, and a job.

The big man, Rob, laughed from his big belly and turned to Sara. "Most people are slowly leaving this sad area. There is no industry here unless you like sheep. There are always salespeople at the grocery stores or waitress at the rest stops. What type of work are you looking for?"

Shrugging Sara looked around at all the older style trucks and vehicles. "I'm a bookkeeper. I usually work for CPAs or someone like that, but I can do accounting anywhere." She decided to put in a good word for herself. One never knew when a job would show up. "I'm a great bookkeeper."

"Bookkeeper." Rob looked around. "You know, if you go 'na stick around, there's a rancher out near Falls Creek who is lookin' for a bookkeeper. Tal Rawan is his name, and he has one of the big spreads. He has a lot of extra businesses and lots of help."

Smiling her friendliest smile, Sara nodded. "I'm hoping to stay, but that depends on a job, a place to stay, and a cheap ride."

With a new friend in a small southwest town that was full of friendly people, it was a week before she met Mr. Rawan, who was obviously an American Indian. He was a handsome man in his mid-fifties or somewhere, as it was hard to tell from his hard tan and dark skin.

Before meeting him, she had two other job interviews. One was at the bank, but it didn't look good at all since they only hired part-time. The other was at the CPA's office, where the woman said she could use help during tax time.

Depending on what happened with her interview with Mr. Rawan, Sara would either stay or move on to another small town in New Mexico. Hopefully, she would not leave any large trail for someone from the mesa to follow.

Mr. Rawan sent word though Rob at the garage that he would like to meet her on Friday for lunch at Mae's Café. There were three restaurants in the small town, and Sara had sampled them, surprised that the food was good at all of them.

As she waited at a table by the window, a tall man with a long black braid walked up and spoke. "Miss Donaldson?"

Sara started to stand, but he spoke immediately. "No, sit down. I'm Tal Rawan, and I love Mae's food, so they know me and will bring me stuff immediately." He pulled out a chair and was soon nodding to several people.

"So Miss Donaldson, do you have a resume and recommendations?"

Sighing, Sara shook her head. "That's going to be a problem. I am on the lam."

The tall man looked at her and then laughed. "What crime did a pretty little thing like you commit?"

Waving her hands, she started over. "No, let me explain. I'm running away from a rich abusive boyfriend. The kind with an ego that doesn't accept *no*."

Now the tall guy leaned back. The light did show a few strands of grey within that black hair, which was pulled away from his face by a braid that went down his back to his belt. "Is he going to show up here one of these days with some muscle to help him?"

"Well, I really don't think so. Besides, his type of muscle is the government, and I don't think they'll get involved in chasing me across the country."

There was silence for a moment as a large platter of food was set in front of the man. The guy put milk in his coffee and some salt on his food and then nodded.

"Okay, some big shot's son with no brains. I know the type. I tangle with the government all the time."

Again silence fell between them, and Sara drank her coffee while Tal dug into his food. She let him eat while she wondered if she should wait or just get up and leave. Sara hated the lies but didn't have the right to share the truth and involve this man in something that was worse.

The waitress came by and topped off their coffee, and he took a break to look up at her. "So, are you a bookkeeper?"

Now Sara could tell the truth. "Yes, a really good one. I have spent the last seven years working for two good CPA firms. I know a lot about the ins and outs of tax problems, and I do double entry with a range of computer programs or entirely by hand, which is slower."

His stare was intense from those dark Indian eyes. Someday she would need to do some research and discover what tribe his ancestors were. Right now, he was a very serious businessman.

"Okay, I will give you one month. The pay is thirty dollars an hour for a forty-hour week. The job also includes room and board, as the job is done out on my main ranch and it is quite a ways out into the country. You won't be able to get into town very often, so you might want to pick up an extra tube of toothpaste. Rob will give you directions."

Unbelievably, the drive out in the cheap four-wheel car that Rob had sold Sara, took seven hours. The directions and map that Rob gave Sara were easy to follow. The narrow roads that eventually turned into unpaved but solid wide dusty routes went up and down gentle slopes that gave long views of the distant mountains that never seemed to get close.

There were strange wooden signs at the unpaved turn-offs announcing what she guessed were ranches. The one pale pick-up that passed her made a big show of everyone waving as if they knew her or they were pleased to at last see a human out on this dry highway.

Following Rob's instructions, she turned off at a wide road without a sign but which did have ruts to indicate it was often that two vehicles passed each other. The dry road was in good shape, and her old car handled well. Rob had not cheated her, perhaps because of Tal. The old car still had AC that worked, and it did not eat up gas. At last, she found the markings of the ranch. It was like something from one of those TV series on oil ranchers. There was a rough wooden fence, if you could call it a fence, with wood posts and lots of barbed wire.

There was a very wide wooden gate that was open with an arched carved wooden sign above that announced Rawan Ranches. Stopping before the open gate, Sara was able to see what must be thousands of sheep, and off in the distance was a collection of buildings.

As she drove closer, everything looked like structures on a southwestern ranch should look. All the buildings were low except for one large barn and the main house. They were painted brown or dark red, and there was a lot of white trim on the buildings, even the barns.

So this was a sheep ranch and a business, and it seemed to be prosperous. People were moving around, and when she pulled past the big ranch house to head toward the busy lower buildings, someone waved her over to one side.

Rolling down her window, she smiled at the grizzled grey-bearded man who walked up. "Hi, I'm the new bookkeeper."

"Oh, sure, the boss said a pretty lady would be here some-time today. Well, I'm Carlin, head of the local section. Let me show you where to park." The man walked around and got into the passenger seat.

"Just go on past the tall barn and along with the long low building." He smiled as he pointed out the way and waved at a couple of people. He had removed the weathered wide hat when he got in and immediately turned the air vent onto his face.

The long low building behind the tall barn looked almost like a motel without any neon signs. There was a long covered porch that ran along the front with doors and windows under its roof. A rough wooden railing that separated the porch from the dusty drive had the look of fresh paint. There were several vehicles, mostly older pick-ups, that were parked nose forward against the railing. To her surprise, in one spot a saddled horse was tied to the railing.

"This is where you'll stay. It ain't bad, as there are AC units and lots of hot water. You're in number eight. Seven has Archie in it, but he is mostly out on the range, and ten is empty, so you will find it quiet."

Carlin helped her move her tote inside as she carried her other large bag and some items she had bought in town. She was surprised to find it a long, deep room with amenities that were unexpected.

The first small room was a comfortable sitting room with a large screen TV and was separated by a bar from a small kitchen behind it, with a refrigerator and pots and pans. Going through the wide door led to a comfortable bed and big closet with finally a bathroom. There was a stand-alone shower, a big bathtub under a high window, and everything else needed to make a person comfortable.

Carlin dropped her larger tote on the floor near the closet and turned around to wait in the front room while she checked everything out. Finally, she stood against the counter, looking over at him.

"Well, your office is in the main house. Everyone walks around here, so I hope you have comfortable shoes or boots. Most of us eat at the back tack kitchen. You can find it by the smell, and the food is pretty good. Of course, you can eat in your room if you prefer privacy.

"Everyone here is safe, so just ask anyone you meet for help with directions. If anyone gives you problems, you report it to me, and we drag them on a rope behind a truck.

"The last thing is what is your name, and what do you like to be called>"

Introducing herself and using her real name, Sara was settled into a room, a job, and had some new friends. True, everything was different—she was hours away from town and any shopping or restaurants. But the ranch took care of most of that for its many residents.

The cook set out a self-serve breakfast and a cold lunch. For those that were working away at lunchtime, there were boxes or bags to fill up so that lunch sandwiches, salads, and fruit were ready to go. Sara soon began to take a bag for her lunch at her computer.

Her office was a clean, neat room in the main house. A woman answered the side door and told her that she was named Molly and she was in charge of the house. Sara wasn't sure what that included for the attractive woman who also looked to be of American Indian descent. She also seemed to be about thirty or thirty-five.

Sara was turned over to a guy who welcomed her to her office and a great computer with the latest accounting program, up to date in its attachments. Unfortunately, there had been no input for about a month, so she had her work cut out for her. The guy was Sefer, another member of the tribe, who said he was in charge of combining Tal's many businesses and investments together here at the ranch.

Sefer took the time to explain what was in the different full plastic folder size holders on the desk. He also explained the different filing cabinets, both in her office and in the very large storage office in the back. Sefer didn't explain what had happened to the previous bookkeeper.

Settling into her work for that first week was easy, as she had a lot to do, and most people left her alone. Oh, everyone smiled and nodded or waved in a friendly way, but it was soon obvious that everyone had a job to do and took their work seriously.

For Sara, until she felt that she knew everyone better, she grabbed a plate of the great food at the outside meals each night and took her food back to her room or apartment, whatever she chose to call the nice place assigned to her. There was no voice in the night.

Missing her talks with Jeff, she began to think that at las, she had gotten too far away for the soldier to be able to talk to her in her dreams. Damn. She did not see her employer, but she found out that she was in charge of the payroll through the system, so Sefer came in with her to walk her through the first time.

It seemed some people got checks, some people got their payroll transferred into their checking or debit accounts, and there were a few who could cash their checks at the ranch. This was discouraged and was offered more for a short term or emergency. So Sara could get her first time as cash if she wanted, but she decided to open a PayPal account and have the funds put into that place immediately.

There would be a few days before her card would arrive, but she could pay bills online and even get funds from the ranch cash immediately. It would work.

After a couple of weeks, Sara was beginning to relax and feel she might have found a place. First of all, everyone she met was relaxed and friendly. They all seemed open, and although they wanted to talk, they didn't ask any private questions.

Although she got some whistles from afar and some offers to go into town, none of the passes were serious or uncomfortable. She soon found herself eating more meals at the back tack kitchen, which was an open setting out under the stars.

CHAPTER FIFTEEN

The man she was working for had an interesting chain of businesses. He seemed to have his hands into a lot of things in many states, including investing in some big companies that got noticed on the stock exchange.

Doing this bookkeeping, she realized he did not need someone of her talent; what he needed was a true accounting firm. This man was a millionaire, hiding out here in the middle of New Mexico.

Well, he wasn't exactly hiding out, since she had not seen him at the ranch from the time of her interview in town. Perhaps he didn't stay here, just kept this place that would not draw attention. He probably had a penthouse in New York or Chicago or even overseas.

In one of the companies she posted, there were a lot of receipts for overseas traveling and purchases. Her office and the house, what she saw of it, had everything one would need, but there was nothing over the top about the equipment in each room. Most of the furnishings were polished wood with leather and a lot of Indian blankets or fur rugs. Thank goodness no animal heads were hanging on the walls.

As for the food that the chef cooked, she discovered that a person could ask for anything. There was a night when Chinese was served, and it was good, from the veggie egg rolls to the noodles. The cook stated it was served on a request.

Everything was going almost too good, except Sara missed the voice in the night. She couldn't help but wonder what had happened up in the mountains above Denver. After all, the project on the mesa was a government operation, and there was a chance that the Army had taken over the town. There still was the fact that a large number of the citizens of Benson had found a way to get out in the same way that Sara had, walking through the forest and down to the highway.

Malcom Brown's CPA service was probably still there and might be open. Sara drummed her pen on the desk as she stared out the window. No, she was not going to be stupid and contact Malcom, or Timmy, who had a taxi that he lived in most of the time.

Putting the pen down, she pulled over one of the plastic stack trays. These black units could lock on top of each other, but she kept them spread out. Each represented a different company or division with a company or the ranch.

Within the accounting program, Sara was able to set up a separate file for each of these, so all she had to do was hit a couple of keys to switch from file to file. It kept the whole idea of bookkeeping from getting boring. Within each folder, she still had to make intelligent decisions. Somewhere there was going to be a CPA who would look at the final recap that showed the totals of all the accounts in each file. What Sara decided was what should go into each account, and that was important as it impacted the tax bite at the time of tax season.

Upon a quick search, she found the CPA's name due to the payment made each year for its services. It was a firm located in Chicago. So her boss preferred the middle of the country over the east coast.

It was a month after she had started her job when two unusual events happened. The first was when she went in early in the morning to her office, and the other was when she settled down for sleep that night.

Starting with the first, she dressed in the comfortable clothes that most of the workers at the ranch wore, either for outside work or in the various buildings, including the big house. She had on boots, jeans, and a comfortable shirt tied at the waist. She wore little make-up and had her hair in a long braid.

She walked into her office with her hands full of coffee, an egg sandwich, and mail under her arm. Paperwork and mail were handed to her by both Molly and Sefer every day that she came through the side door to her office. They didn't warn her that she had someone waiting for her in her workplace.

The tall man with the long dark braid showing traces of grey had his back to her as she entered. Surprised, Sara halted just inside the door and waited.

Tal turned as he looked over the papers he was examining to give her a nice smile. Okay, it didn't look like she was in any trouble so far.

"Good morning, boss."

"No, the name is just Tal. How has everyone been treating you?"

Not wanting to sit down in front of this man, Sara moved to the end of her desk and began to put all of her items down. "Everyone has been great. They have made me feel like a friend and not an outsider. Thank you, sir, er, Tal."

"I see you have added a couple of accounts. My Chicago CPAs had run this." Tal waved the printouts he was holding.

Uh oh, had she gone too far. Was she supposed to ask him or Sefer or Chicago before making any changes?

"Go ahead and take your normal seat and don't look so worried. That frown doesn't go with that pretty face."

With a sigh, Sara moved around and sat down in her good chair and looked up at the tall millionaire boss. She wondered how many American Indians were now millionaires? Times had changed. She had heard about the many casinos on Indian lands in America. Some of them had to have actually put money into the natives.

Wanting to get rid of the frown that Tal had referred to,

Sara asked a question. "How does my work look? Does you CPA service approve of my changes?" She had her fingers in an imaginary crossed position as she waited for his answers.

There was a deep chuckle from Tal as he put the printouts down. "They not only approved, they want to hire you themselves and move you to Chicago. I told them to go to hell. So your trial period is over, and I will give you a raise to keep my friends up north from stealing you."

"Wow, that's great. So I guess I can eat my egg sandwich."

Now the tall man's chuckle turned into a full laugh as he headed out the door. "Back to work. Just because I complimented you doesn't mean you can slack up. See you on my next trip home."

Sitting back with a grin on her own face, Sara reached for her coffee with one hand and hit the keys to turn on her computer with the other hand. Yes, she had learned a lot when working all that time at two CPA offices.

She took a break at lunch and grabbed a salad to eat outside on one of the porches on the many buildings. The weather was hot, but it was dry, and a breeze blew across the flat land to bring the mixed smell of fresh air and animals.

Revived, she went through a lot of papers in the afternoon. As she cleaned up and shut everything down, Carlin stuck his head in the door.

"Hey, pretty lady. The cook is serving early and long into the evening. He is fixing oven-baked pizza. Stop by, and he fixes several varieties with a thick or thin crust. A beer and pizza are only served once a month, so don't miss it." With that announcement, his worn sun face was gone.

Deciding a slice of pizza would top off a great day, she headed for the back tack kitchen that was partially outside with long picnic tables that had been specially built to hold ten or twelve people on both sides.

She ended up eating two slices of thin crust pizza with

sausage and mushrooms. The sauce tasted authentic, and a cool tall glass of beer topped everything off perfectly as she watched the orange sunset and then bright stars appear in the sky.

The table she had been sitting at was full of what at one time would have been called cowboys. Now she wasn't sure what to call the men and women who rode out on horses to tend sheep and cattle, as there were more sheep on this ranch than cattle. They told funny tales on each other, and as the beer flowed, the tales got bigger and a little bit sexy.

Covering a yawn, Sara gave a smiling goodbye to everyone and headed to her own cabin. She passed her own four-wheeler and shook her head. She had not even started it up since driving into the ranch. It was covered with so much dust you could hardly see the color. She made a note to herself that this weekend she needed to start it up to charge the battery and find someplace on the ranch to wash it to let its original color show once again.

Inside, she took a long hot shower and put on a long tee-shirt, then turned down the AC unit and crawled into bed. Turning off the lights, she was always amazed at how dark it was out here away from any lights from towns or cities. Rolling over and burying her head in a nice soft pillow, she closed her eyes.

Hello Sara.

Sara opened her eyes in the dark room. It was Jeff, the first time since she had come to the ranch. She had almost decided that she was too far away for him to reach her.

Are you asleep?

"Yes." Sara felt that she could talk in a low voice in this bedroom, as she had never heard any noises from her neighbors, especially the guy left of her unit who had a different woman every weekend. She found she was mad at Jeff.

Can you safely talk?

"Yes, but I am sleeping."

Even in her mind, she heard him chuckle. *If you are asleep, how can you talk to me?*

"Lots of people talk in their sleep."

Are you mad at me?

"How can I be mad at a voice in my head? Do you know that Son of Sam heard a voice and said it was a dog? You are a dog."

There was silence for a moment, not only in the room, but in her mind. Finally, Jeff chuckled again.

I think you called me a dog so I guess you are pretty angry with me.

Sitting up and putting some pillows behind her and the headboard, she still did not turn on a light. "Where have you been? I have missed you, and I've been worried about you. I have also been worried about the people of Benson. What happened to the town?"

As for Benson, everything is fine. While all the Army was out in the town searching for something or someone, a new Colonel came in via helicopter and ordered everyone back into the Camp. No one was arrested, and nothing was said about so many citizens missing.

Feeling relief sink into her system, Sara relaxed.

"Do you know what started the Army going into Benson? Could they have been looking for me?"

There was the pause as she guessed Jeff was thinking.

I don't know how they found out about you, but I am afraid you might have been involved in their actions.

"Is that why you haven't contacted me?"

I don't know how they could follow our mental contact. I am afraid that they have used others of our special team to figure out a connection. I think there had been others of the project that might have contacted someone outside. They are keeping us under tighter control with more guards and have moved us deeper into the mountain.

"Are they hurting you guys or making you do things you don't want to do?"

Again there was the silence. He probably was thinking about how much he wanted to share with her.

They aren't going to hurt us, as we are their special project that they have invested untold amount of time and staff along with millions of tax dollars. There could be a traitor, or they've watched us closer than we all thought possible.

"And are they watching you now?"

No. I am doing something for them. I am again starting fires. I am making them happy and controlling what I do as I could start much larger fires. We all keep secrets about our powers.

"Great, so now I should worry about how powerful you are when you talk to me?"

Hmmm. I could show you.

Thinking for only a moment, Sara knew she trusted Jeff. "Go for it, big boy." She added her own chuckle.

Suddenly, she gasped as the blanket moved down and her tee-shirt move upward. "What the hell?"

Shhh.

There was a feeling of warmth like a hot breath against her neck as her tee-shirt continued to move up, baring her body.

"Oh, wow." She felt someone's lips moving across her ribs. No, that was impossible. She was finding it hard to get enough air into her lungs. Those lips had found one of her breasts, and now she lost what little breath she'd taken in.

Soft warm lips encircled that tip and pulled in a strong but gentle way as Sara threw her head back above the pillow against the headboard. This wasn't possible, but the feeling of heat was so intense in her body that her mind wasn't working.

Something like hands was pushing against her thighs, separating her legs. Ghost-like feelings of breaths and soft touches like satin floated across her stomach as the lips left her breast to move downward. *This can't be happening. It has to be a dream.* She would wake up and smile at herself for having sex visions in her sleep.

Then the lips were at a place that was most important to

females, and she felt her entire body tense as heat rolled through her body. No, there was no way a man thousands of miles away could bring her to an orgasm, but then the touch was more than soft, and she banged her head as her toes clenched, and all the muscles in her body tightened first, and then everything let go as the orgasm released her.

Chapter Sixteen

It was Saturday, and Sara slept in after the night before with Jeff and an experience of touching over a distance. She had fallen asleep with the most wonderful exhaustion from sexual satisfaction. She wished she had a friend to share this experience with, not that she would tell anyone. No, it was a wonderful secret.

Smiling, she finally got up and put on jeans that she rolled up and dug out a pair of old tennis shoes. It was time to get her old handy four-wheeler looking better and make sure the battery was charged.

Going over to get a light breakfast gave her a chance to ask about buckets and water to wash her car. A couple of guys offered to help, and after she turned down their help, they sent her around the big barn, where they told her that the horses and cattle were washed.

There was indeed one other pick-up being washed, so she parked behind it and got out to talk to everyone to get advice. It seemed the water was recycled for additional washings and to help with the planting in the gardens.

A manager of the barn area said he couldn't get the water management person out, as she was busy down in one of the fields. As he leaned against the front of her dirty hood, he explained how they had to treat the water to get rid of all the soap and anything else that would affect the plants. It was still not fit to drink, but it was perfect for the gardens.

Surprised that her car had started up on the first turn of the key, she was leaving it run as she waited her turn, making sure the battery got its full charge.

Suddenly, there was Jeff's voice in her head so loud it was like having a gunshot right into her brain. She let out a yell and dropped down to one knee, holding her head with both hands.

Run, Sara, run. They are coming for you.

She tried to get to her feet as a couple of the men were moving to help her.

"What happened? Did she hit her head?"

Someone handed her a clean rag, and she realized her nose was bleeding. Pulling away from the men as she was finally on her feet, she looked off to see if there was dust from fast-moving vehicles.

"Let me help you get back to your cabin." One of the men had his arm around her as she struggled to keep on her feet.

"No, I have to get out of here. Wait, I have to get my special away tote in my cabin. Damn." Pulling away from the rustic guys, she used the car as a base and moved to pull the front door open.

"Hey, wait sweetheart. If it is a bully ex, we can protect you. We don't take well to guys that don't treat ladies in a good way."

Shaking her head, Sara couldn't involve these guys. She had to get away from the ranch. "You don't understand. It's not an ex, it's the government."

By that time, someone came around the barn and pointed up into the sky. "Look up, guys. The copters."

Now Sara knew she was done. She might get away across the desert in her four-by-four against a couple of black SUVs. But there was no getting away from a threat in the sky. How had they found her?

An older man seemed to take charge. "Okay boys, there is nothing Tal hates more than government agents, especially on his ranch property. Let's hide this pretty lady. Mark, you strip that car of anything that shows it's hers; and Handley, take a couple of guys over to her cabin and get everything of hers out of it. Treat her stuff gently, but do it fast."

Sara was confused as she looked around, holding the clean rag to her nose. "I need to get away to protect you people, as well as myself."

"Don't worry little lady, we have worked with the bullies from the government before. Tal will get a message and start talking to his senator buddies. In the meantime, you must trust us."

He nodded to the guy in denim and heeled boots standing next to her. "Take her to the lower space in the tack room."

"No, you don't understand. They only want me. If I get in my car and run, they will follow me and leave you guys alone."

"Very brave madam, but we would feel like traitors and not sleep very well if we let those tyrants run off with a help-less female." He nodded at her tall friend.

The guy smiled down at her and just picked her up with an arm under her knees and one around her back to carry her easily around the barn toward one of the long buildings that were built to hold the horses. Even in the heat of the day, as soon as they entered the shade of the large door, the temperature dropped, and it felt cooler.

He let her stand on her own feet, but he still had a firm grip on one upper arm as he headed to a door of a closed-off section. It had a keypad locked entry where he punched in a couple of numbers, and upon hearing a click, he opened the door.

Inside was a large room that smelled of leather and was full of saddles and hooks with reins and ropes and leather thongs. Among the midst of this workroom stood an office desk with papers strung across the top. At last, her friend let go and walked across to push a couple of trestles that held saddles off to one side.

There didn't seem to be any difference in the rough

wooden floor that Sara could see, but the guy stooped over and pushed on a board. It made one end pop up that he could lift and a door was pulled open with his hands to show a dark hole below.

"There are two electric lanterns and here is a flashlight to help you down the steps. Don't make a sound as anyone standing right above in this spot could hear you. I or someone from the ranch will let you know when they are gone."

Looking at the flash he had handed her, she glanced up at him. "I don't think you know what you are getting yourselves into. This involves the Army."

"Well missy, I was in the army, and they never sent me inside the USA to chase after pretty women except on leave in bars. So I do think that we all have an idea that someone is stepping over the laws and crushing them and that is something we don't allow. Now go on down and don't worry. You will be safe."

Maybe these cowboys did have an idea. Maybe if she did hide, the men in the helicopters would go away if they didn't find her and she could come out. Then she would get in that four-by-four and get far away.

Halfway down the steps, she turned on the flashlight and scanned it around. She was surprised to see a furnished room with a cot and a cabinet with a lot of books and a camp light on one small table and another on a chest. It all looked safe, so she slowly made her way the rest of the way down the steps and across to the first camp light and turned it on.

"Will they see the light above?" She watched the face hanging over the opening.

"Nope. Don't worry. When the door is closed, it interlocks tightly, and no light can be seen from below. There are additional batteries in the drawer, but you shouldn't be down there that long."

He disappeared, and Sara thought he was going to close

the door, but she heard him talking to someone. Suddenly two bags were dropped down.

Her buddy's head appeared again. "Handley says the one is from your cabin. He says it looks like a special bag. The other is fresh food and water. If this takes too long, we will find a way to drop more goods. Stay safe and quiet, and trust us."

He gave her a salute and then he slowly closed the door. It took a bit to settle the wood into place. Then there was a lot of noise of scraping, and Sara guessed it was the trestles with the saddles being put back in place.

Standing in the area, it dawned on Sara that she was trapped. God, had she made the right choice in trusting these men? In this restricted area, she needed light, so she went over and turned on the other camp light. It was amazing how bright these lamps were, with a brilliance almost too much to stare at directly.

There was a strange tall orange metal unit in one corner, so she walked over to investigate and found it to be a camping bathroom. It had an easy open handle at waist high, and when she opened it, there was no smell and instructions on the back wall that it flushed with fresh water from a holding tank. That gave her a feeling of relief for being a normal woman.

Going back to the two totes that had been dropped down, she knew what was in the one that had belonged to her. It was her Be Ready to Run tote, and besides simple clothes and bathroom items, it had cash. The other she sat on the cot and began to unload and set on the various shelves and tables. It contain bottles of water, a couple of sandwiches that would be eaten immediately, some ready-made salads, and then there were the things that would last.

There were crackers, cans of meats and tuna with the new small bags of mixed tuna and chicken already with sauce and mayonnaise. There were bars of trail mix and candy of various types, including some that didn't contain sugar. This might not be a bad place to stay.

Sara used the toilet, picked a package of trail mix, turned off one of the lights, and settled down on the cot with her pad. She brought up a book to read with the sound off and had a nice several hours.

What interrupted her reading was noise from above on the wooden ceiling. Actually, she should call it a floor. Shutting off her pad, she wondered if she should turn off the light. Still, the guy that had helped her down here said the light would not show through the cracks up above. Instead, she just lay back and listened to the movement. Someone was stomping to see if there was anything under the wood floor.

In her mind, she could see an officer and some guy in a black suit giving orders and a couple of army men with heavy boots stomping as instructed. It made her smile as she watched a trace of dust fall from one side of her ceiling.

When this was over, and if she wasn't in the handcuffs, she needed to ask one of the ranch guys what the government types looked like and who gave the orders.

Good thing she had dressed comfortably to wash her car, the tennis shoes and the old soft jeans were just right for hiding in a hole in the ground. Sara used the camp toilet one more time and then poured a small amount of water in a metal bowl and washed her hands and face. Her pad told her it was a quarter after nine, so she ate another sandwich, kicked off her shoes, and settled down.

Finding some candles, she lit one near her bed and turned off the brighter light. Sara tucked a flashlight under the small pillow and put a bottle of water on the table beside the cot. Now she hoped she could get some sleep, as she might have to run out on the desert tomorrow. And maybe Jeff would talk to her in the dim light of the candle.

Chapter Seventeen

Waking up in the dark did not surprise Sara, but it did take her a moment to remember where she was and to find her flashlight. The candle had burned down until the wick had gone out after she had fallen asleep. Feeling a little stiff, Sara turned on the bright camp light that was on the table beside the cot.

The first thing was to use the camp toilet. Glancing up at the ceiling, she heard no noise. Pouring water into the wide metal bowl, she washed her face and hands, then dumped the used water into the toilet. Now it was time to look through her stash and decide on breakfast.

Finding what was titled as a Breakfast Bar, she was surprised to discover it was satisfying and washed it down with a bottle of fruit juice. Next, she decided that she needed to do some exercises in the small area, so she determined yoga would be a better choice. It wouldn't bring up a sweat, but it would put a strain on her muscles.

It had been a while since she had participated in the mind and body activity, but she remembered certain poses and took off her jeans. She gave herself an hour, and it went pretty fast.

Sighing as she sat down on the cot, Sara knew it was going to be a boringly long time down in this hole. Going through her tote, she found she didn't have her laptop. So she only had her cellphone and her pad. She knew it was stupid to use her cell, as it could be traced.

She could read mail on her pad, but she couldn't answer or send out letters. She was able to read the news reports and all the novels she had downloaded. She couldn't go online for any reason—that would send out signals that could be traced. At this point, Sara wasn't worried, as she had several books downloaded from her free account. That meant she had plenty to read. There were also plenty of games to play in between novels.

Just as she settled down on the cot with her present story opened, there was a noise above. She sat up and watched the ceiling. There were scraping sounds and boots, and then the door above the steps began to move. Had the soldiers found her hiding place?

Sara was undecided as to what to do next. She had no weapons. Should she turn the light off? Should she hide? There were not many places to hide besides by the metal toilet, and it wouldn't take them very long to find her in that small stinky area. All she could do was turn off her pad and clutch it tightly as she sat and looked upward at the slow opening.

"Hey, pretty lady. It's safe to come out. Come on up." It was the guy that had helped her into the hole. She couldn't even remember his name.

"Okay, thanks. Just a minute." She got up and grabbed her special tote, then stuck the pad into the side pocket. She pulled on her jeans and shoes and started up the steps. "Oh, wait, I should turn off the light."

"No problem. We always check everything out and clean up and restock for the next user." The guy held down a hand to help her. She chose to give him her tote and use both her hands to hold onto the floor to get off the steps and stand up into the room.

Now Sara stood and looked down into the hidey-hole. How long had that hidden room been down there, and how often had it been used over the years? Interesting. What was going on behind the scenes at the Rawan Ranch?

Sara was not one to ask questions about others, since she was running from the government and the Army.

"Ms. Donaldson, I need to take you to the main house. Mr. Rawan flew in last night after all the other 'copters flew out when someone reminded them they were flying over American Indian Reservation property without permission."

The light might be on in the room below, but another went on in Sara's head as she remembered all those accounts on which she'd brought data up to date. Yes, one of the separate financial records was for Reservation Securing. She had taken the word *reservation* to mean something else when it tied in with the natives of New Mexico.

Sara was working on a native reservation, and of course, as she surmised, most of the employees on this ranch were members of the tribe. She had to wonder if she got in her hardy vehicle and drove into the desert whether she would find an Indian village of old houses with beat-up cars in the yards and raggedy dogs barking as she drove past the grassless pastures.

That was what she had seen in recent news releases, except around the casinos. It seemed that the natives didn't work in the casinos, but they did reap the rewards. It was all on reservation land.

All of this was going through Sara's mind as she followed her guide up to the main house. She would have been able to get to her meeting without an escort, but perhaps they were worried that she might leave without talking to the boss.

They went to the front door, and her guide told her that the boss's office was on the left. There were double doors with one open, so she went ahead and stood to wait to see if she was invited into the room.

Tal was sitting in a big leather high back chairs with a portable phone to his ear. He waved Sara to a chair then he gestured to the man behind her for the door to be closed.

"I don't think any federal charges will be filed." Tal was speaking to someone on the phone. He seemed to be waiting for whatever was said on the other end, and then he finished. "Thank you, Senator. I am sure it was all a mistake. I will see you the next time I am in the East." With that, Tal nodded and hung up the phone.

Leaning forward, Tal now had his intense eyes directly on Sara. "So Ms. Donaldson, you brought the Army to my home and to my people who are very important to me. Want to tell me what this is all about?"

Looking down at all of the papers on the large wooden desk, Sara tried to decide what to say in answer to that question. She wanted to tell this man the truth, but some of it would make him think she was nuts. Okay, she would try for the truth with some editing.

"First, I am sorry. I never thought my trouble would follow me here. Let me start at the beginning, but I will keep it short. I want to assure you that I have done nothing against the law. Having done a lot of taxes, I guess I know a lot about what would pass for problems with the Feds."

Still sitting on the front edge of the comfortable chair, she took a second to get her ideas in order. "About almost two years ago, I moved from Florida after my mother died to a small town call Benson in the mountains above Denver. It is not a ski or casino town, so it is dying. The only thing that has happened to it in the last few years of interest is that the government came in and bought some land above the small town to build an Army Camp that was really for some lab work or experimental efforts."

Looking up to meet his eyes to make sure he understood what she was telling in this story. "The Army Camp was isolated, and no one in the town had anything to do with the camp or met anyone within the walls built around the mesa that they had sectioned off for privacy.

"Through a bit of some unusual conditions, I got to know one of the soldiers. Evidently, this was strictly against the rules. My friend is sure that this group is so paranoid that they would just take me and make me disappear if they found out about me. It seems he knew of that happening to others. Now he thinks that they know about me, so he warned me to get away."

Shrugging her shoulders. "I just got on the first plane leaving Denver, and it was going to New Mexico. I thought this was far enough away — so here I am." Sara spread her hands out in front of her and then just clasped them down in her lap.

Looking at her with his dark eyes, Tal rubbed his chin while he was thinking. "Did you know this was an Indian Reservation?"

Raising her eyes, she shook her head. "I didn't even know that there were still reservations around in the US. I know that in Florida there is a casino near my old home that's run by American Indians, but I don't know the details. I just know as an accountant that it is smart of them to get some money back."

Without moving, Tal sat still, staring at Sara as if trying to read her both inside and out. "Do you know the rules between the Federal Government and Indian Reservations?"

"I have no idea of any rules. I guess I suppose the FBI and the Army can do what they want. American Indians just seem to be another group of poor people that are pushed around without any of their own rules, so I am sorry that I have brought this problem down on you." Sara fought back the tears and wondered if she could leave to have the Army chase her somewhere else after she took another flight.

Tal sat back and looked up at the ceiling. "We call ourselves tribes and Indians. All the other names are said by outsiders to be politically correct. Each tribe is an Independent Nation with its own rules and police force.

"There are some that do not have police and depend on local and federal officials for controlling small and large crimes. There are some that have a few officers and still operate with help of local authorities. Then there are some that have their own authority in charge of their reservations.

"In any case, the outside local and federal officials cannot enter without permission. The ones that work with outside help have an agreement that allows open walls, where most of the external authorities can't enter without permission, even with warrants issued by any court."

Now he brought his head and eyes back down to look at Sara. "This reservation is one that is totally independent with its own police force. Two state highways run through the reservation, as it is extremely large and takes over several counties here in New Mexico.

"State Troopers take care of offenders on those highways, but if they stop an Indian, they hold them until one of the Indian Officers show up to take the person into the Indian Affairs Office to stand trial."

Taking in everything he was explaining, she was thinking of the helicopters and the dark SUVs. "So, what happened to the vehicles that came into the ranch the other night?"

Nodding, Tal smiled as he answered her question in a mild voice. "A couple of Indian Officers showed up and kindly helped them off the reservation property. A complaint was filed both with the state and in Washington. Before the complaint was filed, the Army 'copters had already disappeared."

Her body felt so tense that even her stomach ached. How could she get away from these people without hurting someone else?

"Sir, I thank you for your help. I will pack up and get off your ranch as soon as possible."

"You're going to leave the one place where you are safe from the Army and whoever is running the place up where you were at on that mountain?"

Looking around the room and over her shoulder at the closed doors, Sara frowned. "Won't there be a lot of trouble for everyone here?"

Shaking his head, Tal pointed out a window. "They will wait for you to leave and then pick you up. But as long as you are here, you are safe. No one will come onto this property to touch you. Of course, that won't get you out of your work. There are a couple of days accounting for you to get caught up, waiting in your office."

Deciding it would be better not to say anything else, as even a thank you seemed trivial, Sara got up and quietly went out and down the many halls to the side of the large house to the area of the workrooms. She slipped into her chair and brought up her computer. There was no work done because her mind was in turmoil, and her hands were shaking.

Losing track of time and not even remembering what she had thought about as she sat in front of her desk, she was jerked aware as Sefer entered the office.

"Sara, that's the sun setting out there. So it's time to get out of here before all those hungry workers eat up everything. How about I walk with you to the back tack kitchen?"

Looking around, Sara smiled at the man. "I guess I let the time get away. Thanks, but I'm not very hungry."

"Sorry, lady. Orders from the boss, food helps the body and the brain after a stressful time. So the cook has some good stuff and also some simple soup. Let's go."

Even in her tired daze, Sara remembered to shut down the computer and made sure everything was in its proper place on her desk. She followed Sefer out of the side door and over to the outdoor eating area. She did settle on a big cup of chicken soup and coffee even though she thought the cook's strong coffee would keep her awake.

Chapter Eighteen

Knowing she wasn't going to be able to sleep, Sara first put away all of her things again. She wasn't sure what they had done with her stuff while she had been down in the hole, but her rooms had the smell of male aftershave. The guys had gone out of their way to hide the fact that a woman had stayed here.

Taking a long hot shower was next on her list, and it felt better than she anticipated. At last, with damp hair and in her shorts and long tee-shirt, she was in bed with her computer, doing some research on Indian Reservations in America. Over thirty-three thousand results came up. *Wow.*

Can you hear me?

"Oh my God, Jeff. Are you okay?" Sara remembered in her shock of hearing from Jeff to also keep her voice low even though she was excited.

You are talking to a Special Army Lieutenant who has been turned into a weapon, and you are asking me if I am okay. You are the one to be worried about. Are you okay and unharmed?

Closing her computer, Sara looked around the small bedroom and decided no one could hear her. "I am fine. It turns out I'm on an Indian Reservation that takes its independence very seriously. My employer, Tal Rawan, has been on the phone with a Senator who evidently likes the minority votes and has helped. Mr. Rawan is also very wealthy, and this reservation is independent in its own right and has its own police force. I am just starting to learn that it makes them separate from the Federal Government."

I love you and your naivety. Look up assassin on your computer.

Now Sara sat still, not moving and not opening her computer. She understood the message he was giving to her in the one word.

"Are you an assassin?"

I am everything. But believe me, the Army has many trained assassins. Many who might look like American Indians because they come from some of the Indian tribes who are natural for that type of project.

Now Sara couldn't get more frightened if she wanted to, fear had her frozen in place on her bed. Damn, what else could happen to her?

"I don't know what to do, Jeff. I am so scared, and this isn't me. I'm just a bookkeeper. I don't know how to shoot a gun or how to hide."

You are not going to hide, and you don't need a gun. What you need is a map. You are on one of the largest Indian Reservations in New Mexico. I want you to get ready for a nice long car ride.

She couldn't decide if she should get out of the bed or sit still and wait for Jeff to explain what he was talking about. "Are you sending me to Mexico? I don't have a passport."

No. I want you to drive back up to Benson.

Looking up maps was easy. Google was a jackpot of charts, surveys, guides, etc., etc. The first info she drew up was for a route between New Mexico and Denver which also showed some information about parks and — *ta da* — some Indian Reservations in New Mexico.

The ranch wasn't the largest, but the second largest, and when you clicked on it, Google told you about the success of American Indians going into the investment business. Politically correct on the title. As for the investments, things began to fall in place as Sara remembered all the data she entered for the different accounts she handled.

Getting up, she dressed in comfortable clothes and

dumped a few more into her travel bag, including her winter boots, then took it and her small special bag that was always ready out to her four-wheeler. Next, she went into the dark house through the side entrance and turned the lights on in her office.

She spent a couple of hours looking through papers and putting in some important data that she felt would keep Mr. Rawan safe until he got another bookkeeper. Shutting down everything in her office, she left a short note of thanks and resignation on her desk.

There was a glow in the east as the first hint of dawn began to glow over the distant hills. On the ranch, there were some people who got up early and some who were finishing their shift. Grabbing an egg sandwich, a bag lunch, and several bottles of water, Sara went to her car.

"Goin' somewhere, Ms. Donaldson?"

It was one of the men who had helped her get down in the hole. She looked closely at him as the sun came up to highlight his profile. Yes, he was an Indian. Could he be an assassin? No, he could have killed her many times.

"Yes, I need to go north and hopefully pull the Army away from you folks."

"Miss, the Army can't hurt any of us here. Wouldn't it be better to wait it out and see what Tal can do with his pull with his contacts?"

Shaking her head, she slid into the driver's position and rolled down the window so she could still talk to the man. "I also have to help a friend up north. He has helped me a lot, and I owe him a debt."

Now the man stepped back and looked up at the last of the stars as they were disappearing. "Ah, a debt must always be paid. Indians believe it is bad to die with debts owed."

Thinking for a moment, Sara realized she did need some information. "I need to get off the reservation and onto the big highway going north. The problem is that the Army and cops probably have all the main roads blocked waiting for me to leave. Is there a way I can get off the reservation without being arrested or captured?"

Nodding, he waved for her to wait as he moved over to one of the outbuildings. It wasn't long before she heard the loud noise of an off-road motorbike. A young man dressed in colorful bike riding leathers roared out and pulled up next to her window.

He looked at her vehicle, even down at the front wheels. "Keep it in four-wheel drive, as we are going off-road. It will be over two hours to get you above the exits they are guarding."

He took off, and she understood that he was leading her off the ranch through the desert. There didn't seem to be a road, but the high chassis on her vehicle cleared the ruts and brush easily as she followed the bike. Looking in her rearview mirror, she was worried about the dust that rose up behind them.

After about an hour, the rider stopped and waved her over. "Need to pee? If so, you can go on the other side of your car, I will give you privacy."

She smiled at the young man as he pulled up the dark visor to show a face of someone who couldn't be over fourteen years of age. He also had the dark eyes and strong nose of an Indian, a member of the tribe.

"Thanks for the offer, but I have a strong bladder." Sara laughed. "But I am worried about the dust trail we are leaving. Won't someone see that if they are watching up high?"

The kid was sipping one of those high vitamin drinks and swept his hand around. "Strange thing happened last night. A bunch of horses got loose. There are a whole bunch of bikers, four-wheelers, and trucks out all over the desert looking for those broncos. We are just one of the groups hoping to get those expensive babies back before the boss kicks us all in the ass."

Laughing, Sara pulled out a bottle of water for herself. "Is Tal that tough a boss?"

"Not Mr. Rawan. He never interferes with ranch business. The tough guy is the foreman. Time to move on."

It did take them another full hour before they came over a small hill covered with sagebrush. The bike went through, and Sara drove over and sighed with relief to find an unpaved road with some standard poles and the wires at the top going off into the remote dunes.

The kid just waved at her to turn left as he spun around, kicking up dust as he went back over the dune.

Okay, she was on her own, but it was a road. It was a little rough, but after driving over the desert, she felt she could handle the ruts in an actual road. She kept the vehicle in four-wheel drive and drove moderately. This kept the dust down and allowed her to watch for any surprises.

Maybe she was too cautious, as the only thing that interrupted her trip on this back road was a long-eared rabbit. Late in the afternoon, still on the road by herself, she made a pit stop. She took some tissues and walked just a few steps to the side; after all, she had not seen anyone on the entire drive.

Back inside the comfortable air-conditioned seat, she made a note to send a thank-you to the man who sold her this older vehicle that was working so excellently. She also needed to thank someone who had topped off her gas tank. This was going to be a long trip back to Benson, almost five hundred miles.

There would be good highways, but according to the map that was upon her phone and talking to her, there were towns and cities. That meant traffic that might make her trip longer. Still, the line on the original map she'd pulled up on her computer did seem pretty straight north with only a few wiggles that went off the course she had set to get to Benson.

Her main decision was whether she should drive straight through or find a motel to get some sleep.

Chapter Nineteen

Ending up staying in a motel on the south side of Denver, Sara remembered the long twisting road up to Benson. She wanted to be rested before tackling that drive up the mountain. She also hoped that Jeff would talk to her, but she did not feel his touch in her mind that night.

Waking up early the next morning and still with no contact with Jeff, Sara grabbed some food from the breakfast set up in the small lobby and went to the nearest gas station to also fill up her car. Then it was onto the highway bypass around Denver and up the strange highway that eventually led to Benson.

On this road, nothing had changed. It was like reliving a dream as she remembered her first time driving up the mountain. She saw the section of the highway that was four lanes going slowly upward. It eventually turned into the two-lane paved road with the pull-overs. She now knew that the pull-overs were for vehicles that met wide loads. The rule of the road was if the wide load was coming down, the vehicles coming up had to back down until they came to a wide area to pull over and let the wide load pass. The pull-overs were also used when the road was covered in heavy snow and some cars got stranded. Cars sometimes would be pushed to the side to be left until a thaw when the cars could be rescued. The drivers would be in the next vehicles traveling through the snow.

Smiling at the mailboxes, she now recognized some of the names as clients of Brown's services. At last, there was the battered sign that announced the town's name.

BENSON POPULATION 15,7 _ _.

Someone had drawn through the last numbers and made them unable to be read.

The town was as she had first seen it, closed businesses and not many people on the street. It was a Thursday, so some of the companies should be open. Then she saw Timmy drive by in his Taxi. He gave her a wave as he went by in his usual slow speed. So some of the usual people had stayed in the town when the exodus happened.

Pulling over to the curb, Sara sat in the vehicle and wondered what she was supposed to do, now that she was here. She thought about Rose, but even if Rose had returned, which was doubtful, Sara no longer had a room at that location.

There was a knock on the passenger window, and Sara jumped. It was just Sam, the kid from the market. She pressed the button to roll the window down.

"Hi, Ms. Donaldson. How you been? It's been real quiet around here with everyone gone."

"Hi, Sam. I'm fine. I was just wondering what happened while I was away?"

The kid grinned as he glanced around. "Well, everyone left."

Chuckling, Sara leaned over to talk to Sam. "So I guess that left you here with only the old men and the Army."

"Oh, the Army is changed. Everything is different up on the mesa." The kid looked up toward the mountain where the camp was located.

It took a second for Sam's words to sink in and then Sara's eyes also went up the road although there was nothing to see but the usual tall trees. "What do you mean? Did the Army get in the black SUVs and drive away?"

Shrugging, Sam leaned into the window. "Nope. Whatever they were doing up there just blew up. It shook the town so much, half the windows were broken."

"So who or what is up there now?"

"Oh, Miss, there is a mess. There are a few soldiers who are going through the wreckage, trying to find out what happened. They have come into town to ask questions. They acted nicer than the ones who were there before and didn't act like they were going to arrest anyone. The thing is, none of us had any information for them."

Pointing over her dashboard, Sara had a frown. "So, what would happen if I drove up there now?"

"Don't know. Some others have gone up and looked around and even came back with souvenirs. Evidently, you can get into the grounds."

With that, she waved goodbye and drove away. She kept her speed low so that she could still see the last of the town and the few people. Sam was right, as she did notice more boarded up windows that must have been broken by some unusual outburst up on the mesa. All the windows that were damaged were the ones on the north sides of buildings.

The streets and alleys were all cleaned up—clearly, there were still enough people around to have cleaned up and taken care of the windows.

Driving out of town, she began to see damage to the tall strong trees. At first, it was just a lot of limbs down, but as she got farther up the clean wide road, there were trees down. At last, as she approached the area that held the wall and fencing, the trees were snapped, and where there were a few standing, they had been stripped of any leaves and smaller limbs.

She slowed as she approached. It was strange to see the damage that happened to what was once a new strong wall. Parts of it were crumbled with gaps, and in other places, the wall was gone. The blocks and wire had disappeared.

What she had been told were double gates at the entrance was only a couple of standard self standing roadblocks with some soldiers standing at ease behind the white and red painted boards. Deciding this was as far as she could go, she stopped and looked around, trying to figure out how to turn around. While she was trying to make her decision, one of the soldiers was approaching her car.

He waved for her to pull over, and she didn't have an option. Sara kind of crossed her fingers and stopped the car, waiting with her window down.

"Can I help you, Miss?"

"Oh, hi. No thanks. I used to have a friend up here, but I'm sure he moved out with most of the rest of the Army." Sara couldn't make up her mind what else to say. He looked like a private.

"May I see your driver's license and car registration, please?"

Trying not to show too much hesitation as she dug out the paperwork, she looked over at the man in uniform with a weapon on a sling around his shoulder. "Is there a problem? I didn't mean to trespass. I was looking for a place to turn around and go back to town."

The soldier was not listening to her as he was reading her license and speaking into a mic attached to his head and ear. The soldier nodded and listened and then looked at her closely.

"Miss, you are approved to go forward onto the base. Lt. Michelson is expecting you. Just go straight until the road drops into a hole then take the path left. This high vehicle will be able to take that path with the potholes. Go to the temporary tents. Lt. Michelson will be watching for you."

Realizing that she was sitting with her mouth open, Sara sat stunned as the soldier was trying to give her back her papers. Jeff was alive. Whatever had happened up here on the mesa had let him live through the eruption. Finally, with shaking hands, she took her papers and drove through the opening that the two soldiers created as they moved the boards.

Chapter Twenty

The shock of the hole at the end of the wide road was an understatement, given what the soldier had told her to watch for to make her turn. The clean paved road was cut off as if some large beast or giant tool had just come down out of the air and took a bite out of the road. What was left was a hole that was about one mile across and deep enough to lose a multi-storied building in it, if something was in the depths.

Nothing was in it except for a small amount of water at the very bottom. If at night someone drove off the road, their vehicle would be lost as it tumbled end over end to finally stop so far down at the bottom of the hole.

Where she sat in her taller vehicle, she could see across it to the sheared off stone of the mountain on the other side that was smooth rock down into its depths. Where did all the dirt, rocks and buildings go that had stood there? She jerked her mind back to her instructions and turned to follow the path that had been cut by many vehicles across the field toward some tents.

Driving to the large dark shelters set up together in what had probably been a vast open area before the accident, Sara found other vehicles. Now there were a couple of helicopters and many Humvees in different modified forms. As she slowly pulled up into a very busy area with a lot of soldiers, she was able to take in a deep breath of relief.

Standing in front of a tent that had large flaps pulled back was Jeff in his full casual uniform. His collar was open at the neck, and a tan undershirt covered that small gap. *So, this is what the Army looks like when in the field in dark tan boots. Yep, he's a soldier and a real warrior.*

Although she had seen him in a uniform once before, it had all been in a haze of love and lust. This time she took a longer look at his last name over the right breast and the word U S Army over the left side. For Sara, she did see his identification of Michelson, but she didn't need the name. She just needed to see the dark eyes.

There was something else that surprised her. He must not be under arrest or in trouble, as there was a solid looking weapon in a holster that was strapped to his leg.

Before Sara could even get the door open, Jeff came over smiling and was offering to help her out of the car.

"I'm so glad you got my message and could come up to meet with us. This shouldn't take very long. Besides, I want you to meet some of my friends." Jeff looked down at her with a smile on his lips, but a serious frown around his eyes.

Okay, she could play this game. In some way she had gotten a message, so she could assume it didn't matter where she had been when she received hearing him in her head. On the other hand, she did believe he didn't want to talk about the fact that they talked from long distances without cellphones any more than she did, not knowing how others would react to that fact.

As he stood by her, he did take a message from something hooked to his ear and another unit attached to his shoulder. He stepped away as he spoke, and she looked around at the Humvees. There were some in sand color and some in a darker color. She had never seen these being driven through Benson when she was working at Malcom's. As the kid in Benson had said, things had changed.

Besides this large tent and another, there were also several small tents set up in neat rows. Everything was obviously placed as far away from the strange hole as was practical within the broken wall enclosure. Other soldiers were hurrying from place to place as if important things needed to be finished immediately. Off in the distance, there was one block building still standing that had some small damage to the end facing in the direction of the hole.

"Sorry about that, Sara. Let's go in, I want to introduce you to some friends." Jeff had turned and was holding out his arm for her to take so that he could escort her into the first tent.

"Jeff, is there some special reason why I am here on this Army Camp?"

He smiled as he moved her slowly through the entrance of an area that was set up like a group of desks and work areas. With her hand hooked in his elbow, she went where he was headed, and they ended up in front of several soldiers sitting and standing before some long tables with what looked like debris spread out, being inspected.

"Sara, I want you to meet my colleagues, Cliff, Dale, and the ugly one is Trace." The three soldiers stepped forward with big smiles. Trace held out a hand to shake, and actually, he looked young and cute. Cliff looked to be the oldest of the four with a few wrinkles in his tan around his eyes. Dale had the face and the build of a soldier just like Jeff, which meant that they all looked a little bigger and tougher than most men.

"So, you are the little lady that finally tamed our L. T." This was from Trace in a low voice. Maybe the whole conversations were going to be a little quiet.

"Oh, it wasn't so much of taming as agreeing on what we both liked and when we could find time to enjoy those things." She shook the hand firmly, having learned from business over the years the right way to handle a grip.

Jeff pointed at some soldiers behind them who were bringing in some other small items. "We are the few lucky ones when whatever it was blew up in the back laboratory. Unfortunately, there are only seventeen of us that lived through the explosion."

"Sir, we need to get back to the search." This came from Trace.

"Right. You three go back and help do what you can. Watch out for the new guys and see that everything is itemized. CID will want a full accounting." With these words, he turned back to Sara and held out a hand. No elbow this time, it was holding hands like two lovers, and Sara needed that closer touch.

"I'm sorry, but I need to take you over to the other big tent to talk to some officers from the CID. They are the ones who investigate when Army personnel are killed. There have been a lot of Army and civilians that were killed when something caused that hole."

They both glanced over to the dark gap that could be seen between a pair of tents. Keeping ahold of her hand, he took her into the next big tent that was mostly broken down into different sections of desk and work areas, like offices.

Jeff introduced her to a Captain Sornson, who was pleasant but businesslike, as he dismissed Lt. Michelson. So she was left with cops who were Army and worried about her special contact with Jeff. Her real surprise here was that most of these people were dressed in normal civilian clothes. They had suit jackets off and their ties loosened with the top buttons of the dress shirts open.

Her conversation with the CID was short and not intense ,as she could answer the Captain's questions easily, and then it was interrupted with news of some different cops on their way into the camp. She got the feeling the Captain saw no reason to share her queries with someone else. Again she felt that need of the Army to close ranks and protect its own.

When she walked out of the tent, her special old car was waiting right in front, with Jeff behind the wheel.

"Get in, I know a back way out."

Without hesitation, Sara opened and got into the passenger

seat, and Jeff took off before she even had the door shut. So they didn't want her talking to whoever was coming through the front gate. Well, that was okay with her. She wanted to avoid any more questions.

A couple of the men in the CID casual civilian clothes waved at the back of the tent as they went by, bouncing over some unpaved route on the grass and ground. Then the ride settled down, as Jeff had the vehicle on an unpaved path that passed several Humvees parked off to the side. At last, they came to the broken wall where there was a cleared area that showed it once had been a gate.

Jeff got out, and since her SUV had such a large compartment between the front seats, Sara got out and walked around to take her place behind the wheel.

Leaning on the open door, Jeff looked back at the mesa. "Just go left and follow the road. It will lead you to the main entrance and then down to Benson. Go on down to Denver and find a nice hotel on the west side of town. I will contact you tonight and try to answer all of your questions." He leaned in and gave her what she needed. It was a long warm kiss.

"Don't worry, Sara. This will soon be over." He closed the door and stepped back to wave her on through the opening.

It took her most of the day and into late evening to pass through Benson and weave her way down the long curving road to get to the bottom of the mountain. To keep from thinking, she had her window open and the radio playing music very loud.

Paying no attention to the name on the hotel, she gave them a credit card and took her two bags up to find a large quiet room. It was what she needed, after all the driving. The bathroom was bigger than most, and she spent a long time soaking in a tub and then used the robe that was hanging on the back of the door.

Splurging, she ordered room service, surprised that the restaurant was still open and she could have more than she needed. Stuffing herself and watching the news that had nothing about a problem up on the mountain, she finally put on her favorite long tee-shirt and shorts and stretched out in the bed. It was past midnight before she felt the brush of Jeff in her mind.

Are you safe and okay now?

Whispering, she answered him. "I am comfortable and in a nice hotel. I think I can talk without a problem as I can't hear the people on either side or out in the halls."

I think the CID people forgot to tell the other folks with all the government initials that you were available for a conversation. The FBI sent some people into Benson to ask around, not that anyone there will have any answers. Mountain folks are very quiet when it comes to the government.

"Jeff, are you four safe? Who will come looking for you from Washington? There must be other records."

Well, that is part of the reason we decided to act the other night. It seems the project leaders decided we were almost at our peak, and they wanted to be the heroes and introduce us to the big guys. They had just one more thing to try.

"Jeff, what happened? I mean, can you tell me anything?"

There was silence for a second or two, and then Jeff was there with a mental sigh.

We corrected a wrong. We wiped the slate clean.

"By making a big hole?"

We needed to make sure there was nothing that told what they were doing and no record of the four of us that would tell anyone that we were part of the project.

"By making a big hole? Do you know exactly how many people were in that area when everything disappeared?"

Even though we were careful to make sure that only those who were involved with our pain were inside the area that disappeared, we all will be haunted by each one that went up with that great amount of rock. I will count them in my nightmares for years. There were 6 surgeons, 4 anesthesiologists, 5 surgical assistants, 11 nurses, 7 bone specialists, 2 metal structuralisms, 8 physical thera-pists. Do you want me to go on? It totaled one hundred eighteen. It could have been one hundred and twenty, but we tricked two jani-tors and got them out of one of the buildings at the last minute.

The number went through her head a couple of times. That many people died all at the same time as a great hole opened up in the ground and side of the mountain.

"So, where did you four guys send all that mud and the buildings?" Sara thought about some big splash occurring off some South Pacific island.

It went as dust out into space. As far as we know, it is still mov-ing away from the sun.

"This is too much for me to take in, as I'm imagining astro-nauts sneezing from fine powder." Sara was glad the room was warm as she shivered and slid down between the blan-kets. "Jeff, when can we be together?"

It finally looks like in a few days they are going to release every-one who was on duty up here at the camp for a few days. The four of us will be able to come down to Denver and get some R&R.

CHAPTER TWENTY-ONE

It was seven months later, and Sara was waiting outside an Army Camp in Kentucky as Jeff and his three friends were being let out for a month on leave. Sara had a beautiful ring on her finger, and they were going to be joined by Trace's new fiancé.

This Army Base was titled US Army Recruiting Center and was one of the older camps in the country. During the Korean and Vietnam wars, it had been a busy place training young men that were at the front of the lines to see the enemy.

Recruits were brought here from all across the east coast as far as Ohio down to Oklahoma. Jeff had not told her why his team had been transferred here, but there were a lot of other things done on the large base besides training new soldiers. Sara decided Jeff would be glad to be away from the cold mountains and into the gentle hills of this area.

Waiting in a large shaded parking area that was designated for civilians, Sara sat in a rented Escalade. She wasn't used to the oversize expensive vehicle, but Jeff had said they wanted something comfortable for all six of them since they were also picking up Trace's girlfriend.

The four men came out, and when she saw them out of uniform, she smiled. She started the car and drove over to pick them up with their large military totes.

Jeff kissed her as he encouraged her to move over and let him drive. That caused a lot of teasing, and the trip started on the light side. They went into Cincinnati and picked up Trace's friend Margaret.

They found a big hotel on the Ohio River and spent a week simply relaxing and having fun. For Jeff and Sara, it was smiling at each other a lot during the day and having smiles from each other's bodies during the night. It was like a honeymoon. Some topics were not mentioned as the six of them went on walks or fishing and on casino boat rides on the big river.

No one talked about Colorado or anything that any of them did when they were assigned to that Camp. The men did talk about other places they had been attached to, overseas, and some dangerous places. These men had been in Afghanistan and Iran. They had put their lives on the line.

Sara decided they deserved to forget the pain inflicted on them by the people involved in the project upon the mountain. She was willing to forget everything that had happened above Denver, including a strange hike down through the forest.

There was no way that she would ask anything more about the talents given through pain to Jeff and the other three men. She smiled as she lay in his arms at night before another planned outing. Perhaps their talents had faded or disappeared, and they were now just average brave soldiers. The next day they had a short road trip planned to an Indian Burial Grounds on the Ohio side of the river.

They had already looked up the location and had plenty of time for the pleasant drive and have a picnic at the location that was really nothing more than some hills where the Indians had buried some of their ancestors.

This time they had stayed on the Kentucky side of the river in a nice Bed and Breakfast, so they drove over a beautiful bridge that had been built into a very high arch. At the top of the bridge, everyone had a view of the hills of Kentucky and the river. It was a great way to start their day trip.

The street through Cincinnati was easy and quick, and then they were on the unusual narrow highway that followed the river west. The highway alternated between views of the river on one side and on the other two different extreme sights. The highway was built on flat areas at times to show farms tucked in valleys, and next there were walls of rock where sheer straight cliffs had been cut to allow the highway to move onward. This allowed the big trucks to move on the narrow road.

Of course, there were some places where there were traces of rocks that had fallen down from the rough cuts into the craggy hills. The six in the luxury car of GMC was relaxed and looking across at the view of the river and the stacks of a power station down below. At this point in the highway, they were high up on the carved out roadway.

"Damn." This was from Jeff as he pulled the big SUV to a stop behind a line of other vehicles. The people ahead of them were either getting out of their cars or were already out and moving forward around a slight bend. Seeing that they were not going anywhere, Sara and those with her got out, as Jeff led them around the cars. It wasn't long before they heard excited voices, and they could see the first signs of an accident.

What Sara saw of the crash was too confusing to understand, what with the stopped vehicles and some people who were moving around. At last, as she got closer and slid sideways to peer past the crowd of nervous yelling people, she understood the problems. Several cars had been involved with a rockslide that had come down from a straight cut up into a hill to make the highway.

A few cars had slid into one after another, unable to stop fast enough as the slide came down fast. That was not the serious problem. One car had been pushed out to the edge with a large boulder and many small ones holding it in position. Beyond it was another, teetering with the front wheels off the edge and some moving stones and rocks around the back.

People were trying to reach or climb out to the stranded

family van. The fact was that there were children and injured adults in that dented vehicle in danger of going over the cliff.

Men were trying to climb over the loose boulders to get to the van, putting themselves in the place of being swept over with the wobbling van. Now everyone began to back up as an unusual occurrence began to happen. It was as if the whole rockslide was shifting, coming towards the people and the stranded cars on this side of the highway.

The people around the man who was pulled from the first partially buried car began to help him move backward as more debris began to cover his vehicle. It was strange, as it looked like everything was moving sideways, and that didn't make sense for such a weight on the road.

Sara looked around as people ran past her and she grabbed Margaret by the hand, so they both turned together to run back to their SUV. She looked around for the men, and it was then that she saw the four big guys standing close together, watching the unusual movement of van and car and rocks. They were the only ones not running away to safety.

There was nothing unusual to see about them, no muscles were standing out on their faces or bodies. There was no glow or aura, it was just that they did not seem afraid of the rocks and what was happening with all the tons of weight that were moving around the van and damaged highway. The noise level was rising along with the dust that was flowing out and covering the road and the people that were running past Sara as Margaret pulled on her hand.

Letting go of Margaret as the girl pulled away to be swept up with others who were running, Sara stood and watched the dust envelope the four guys and eventually enclose her in a white veil.

It took them hours to get their car turned around and past the rescue vehicles and the police cars. They all needed a shower, and their clothes were crusted with dirt and grime.

There was no conversation as they all thought about the people that had been hurt in the strange rock explosion.

The emergency rescue teams had all spoken of the rock jams on the road being a regular occurrence. This one seemed to be a bigger one and would take a lot of work to clear up from both sides of the highway.

The six in the Escalade were quiet on the drive back to their hotel. By the time they pulled into the parking lot, it was late, and they were all tired and dirty. Everyone separated with small quiet goodnights.

Up in their room, Sara disappeared in the bathroom, needing a long hot shower and to think about what she had witnessed. Jeff was waiting for his turn as she came out in a bathrobe. She went to the large bed and stretched out without taking off the robe. It seemed that Jeff also desired a long shower and time to think as she heard the water run in the other room.

He came out in a style that would take the breath away from any female for miles around. He had on only loose PJ bottoms low on his hips and a towel around his neck. His short black hair was still wet, but his shoulders were stiff as if he was ready to fight with anyone in the room. Since she was the only person in the room, she decided a smile would be the better action.

Returning with his own crooked smile, he tossed the towel and came to stretch out at her side, lying on his back with one arm behind his head. At last, he spoke in his low voice.

"You saw what we did." It was just a statement, not a question.

Sara sighed. "Yes. I guess over the last few weeks everything had felt so normal that I had hoped that your talents disappeared with the hole in Colorado. Now it seems I am Lois Lane living with Clark who sometimes is a superhero."

"Sara, we have all tried to forget what they did to us up in that lab buried under the mountain. Even though they might have given us some magic traits, the pain that we endured has left us feeling used, and less than human. We all agree not to be weapons. So we are doing everything we can not to use those powers, to forget them altogether."

He rolled over to look at her, and she now could see the look on his face. There was a mixture of pain and anger. He ran his free hand over her face. "Don't bring this up and try to forget it. You are going to be spending a lot of time with clumsy old Clark. That superhero will probably not show up very often, and never where anyone can see or tell others about a red cape."

He pushed over and gave her a long deep kiss. Not one from some mythical beast, just a sexy smooch from a real man.

The End — or perhaps another Story

About the Author

The author lives in Florida and under the pen name of M. Garnet (Muriel Garnet Yantiss) spends all her time writing, reading or talking to writers and readers.

She writes SciFi, Fantasy, and Adult Romance. Her web site is www.mgarnet.com to show all the books she has written.

She loves to hear from you at mgarnet2@yahoo.com. She answers all emails.

Put in a word where you found this book to let others know how you liked this story. Thanks.